If t...

She ...

In these contemporary twists on classic fairy tales from Harlequin Romance, allow yourself to be swept away on a jet-set adventure where the modern-day heroine is the star of the story. The journey toward happy-ever-after may not be easy, but in a land far away, true love will *always* result in their dreams coming true—especially with a little help from Prince Charming!

Get lost in the magic of...

Their Fairy Tale India Escape
by Ruby Basu

Part of His Royal World
by Nina Singh

Cinderella's Billion-Dollar Invitation
by Michele Renae

Beauty and the Playboy Prince
by Justine Lewis

All available now!

Dear Reader,

What would the world be without fairy tales? Those classic stories we all grew up loving are such a huge part of culture and worldwide lore. I wrote this book as a nod to one of my personal favorites.

Prince Eriko Suarez finds himself in need of rescuing after his boat is capsized at sea. His rescuer happens to be an enchantress he could swear appeared to him as a mermaid. Arielle Stanton can't believe the drowning man she pulled out of the water is an honest-to-goodness prince.

So begins their fairy-tale romance as they fall in love.

I hope you enjoy their story.

Nina Singh

Part of His Royal World

Nina Singh

HARLEQUIN

Romance

Recycling programs
for this product may
not exist in your area.

ISBN-13: 978-1-335-59654-3

Part of His Royal World

Copyright © 2024 by Nilay Nina Singh

For questions and comments about the quality of this book, please contact us at CustomerService@Harlequin.com.

Harlequin Enterprises ULC
22 Adelaide St. West, 41st Floor
Toronto, Ontario M5H 4E3, Canada
www.Harlequin.com

Printed in U.S.A.

Nina Singh lives just outside Boston, Massachusetts, with her husband, children and a very rambunctious Yorkie. After several years in the corporate world, she finally followed the advice of family and friends to "give the writing a go, already." She's oh-so-happy she did. When not at her keyboard, she likes to spend time on the tennis court or golf course. Or immersed in a good read.

Books by Nina Singh

Harlequin Romance

A Five-Star Family Reunion

Wearing His Ring till Christmas

How to Make a Wedding

From Tropical Fling to Forever

Spanish Tycoon's Convenient Bride
Her Inconvenient Christmas Reunion
From Wedding Fling to Baby Surprise
Around the World with the Millionaire
Whisked into the Billionaire's World
Caribbean Contract with Her Boss
Two Weeks to Tempt the Tycoon
The Prince's Safari Temptation

Visit the Author Profile page
at Harlequin.com for more titles.

To RJ, a true prince of a man

Praise for Nina Singh

"A captivating holiday adventure!
Their Festive Island Escape by Nina Singh
is a twist on an enemies-to-lovers trope and is
sure to delight. I recommend this book to anyone....
It's fun, it's touching and it's satisfying."

—*Goodreads*

CHAPTER ONE

Prince Eriko Rafael Suarez had to get away. He couldn't stand one more minute under the same roof as his family. He loved them, he really did. But sometimes they could be a bit...well, much. Especially about his need to eventually succeed his father on the throne. Recently, it seemed his ascension was all the king wanted to talk about. The conversation at breakfast this morning had Riko approaching his breaking point. So he'd made his excuses and left before the second serving of coffee.

Now, he made his way down the sandy beach toward the dock. He was breaking all sorts of protocol. He'd slipped his bodyguards' attention and hadn't told anyone where he was going. Doing so would have only invited argument and the insistence that someone else join him. When all he wanted was solitude and a few moments of peace, sailing on the wide-open sea.

Still, maybe he should have notified Manny of his intentions. His twin could often be the proverbial thorn in Riko's hindquarters, but he'd always been trustworthy.

Too late now. Riko had no intention of going back to the castle and in his haste to get away, he'd left his cell behind. Besides, there was no need to tell anyone what he was up to. He was an experienced sailor, having manned boats since he'd been a preschooler. He even raced competitively once or twice a year. Plus he'd be back in no time.

The sky above was clear and sunny, the wind a gentle breeze and the waves of the water lapped gently on the beach. It was the perfect time for a quick sail. It would be a sin to waste such an opportunity.

Within minutes, he was off, guiding the cruiser smoothly over the water, the shore growing distant behind him. Right away he felt the tension slowly leaving his tight shoulders, the knot of frustration in his gut gradually loosening. Being on the water always had this effect on him. Nature's therapy.

The enormous responsibility of the future that awaited him wasn't lost on Riko. Did his father, the king, really not see that? Of course, Riko knew all that responsibility would land on his shoulders within a few short years. He knew he would have to get married and start a family. His people expected it of him. They expected a royal family to replace the current one on the throne. It was essential for the stability of the kingdom. A smooth transition to the throne was an absolute, following centuries of history.

Not for the first time in his life, Riko had to marvel at the utter randomness of it all. The slight twist of fate that had him being born mere minutes before his twin brother. A humorously short period of merely 120 seconds that settled the very history of Versuvia and made him the firstborn son of the king and hence the heir. In her usual manner of efficiency and competence, the queen had delivered both the heir and the spare within the same small window of time.

Riko gave his head a shake and inhaled the salty sea air deeply. Later. He would worry about all of that later. Heaven knew, he'd be back at the palace soon enough to face his responsibilities. Right now, he just wanted to enjoy these precious moments of solitude.

But Mother Nature apparently had other ideas.

If Riko was a superstitious man, he might have figured some cursed form of magic had brought about what happened next. A thick gray cloud appeared in the sky not far from where he'd anchored, seemingly out of nowhere. After drifting like a stealth plane across the sky for several minutes, it dropped like a rock directly over the boat. Riko could only stand frozen to the spot, watching helplessly. Then the heavens opened up. Torrents of rain dropped like mini golf balls, pounding against his cheeks and forehead. His hair plastered against his scalp. A claw-shaped bolt of lightning lit up the now darkened sky, followed moments later by a sudden crack of thunder that split the air.

The shock of it had him stunned.

But only for a moment. Riko's expertise and training finally kicked in. With the waves growing larger by the second, he knew he couldn't stay anchored much longer. He was bound to take on water. Or worse.

Fighting against the wind and the punishing rain, Riko pushed his way across the deck. Wasting no time, he lifted anchor and ran across the deck to the wheel. It was like wrestling with a sea monster. Riko exerted every bit of strength he could muster to try and turn the wheel to give the sailboat a chance against the blustering wind and violent waves attacking the craft. He knew there was no way to steady her. He just had to keep her afloat and try to take on as little water as possible.

Streams of sweat ran down his face, mixing with the wetness from the pounding rain. The muscles in his shoulders and upper back cried out in protest at the strain. As an ardent gym enthusiast who made sure to put in regular punishing workouts, the strain of effort surprised him. He didn't have time to dwell on it. The next instant, a powerful wave surged toward the boat. Riko gritted his teeth and braced his feet on the deck preparing for impact. The boat was almost completely on its side. Nothing to do now but pray to the gods above that somehow it righted itself.

How stupid of him not to have worn a life jacket. But it had been such a clear day with the water so smooth. And he hadn't intended to be out here long. None of those were excuses for how unprepared he was. And how foolhardy of him not to have told anyone where he'd be or what he'd be doing.

For one spirit lifting moment, the boat appeared to be righting its position. It didn't last. Another massive wave rose out of the water, and Riko knew there would be no escaping this one. He managed to reach for the flotation ring hanging by the wheel just as the monstrosity of water came crashing down.

What came next felt as if it were happening in slow motion. The primitive part of his brain suddenly went on high alert, trying to process exactly how much danger he was in. All in all, he was a fairly competent swimmer, but he'd never swum in weather even remotely this dangerous. As far as visibility went, he couldn't see past the bridge of his nose. His only hope was to swim to the nearest shore, which he would guess was Majorca at this point. Whatever he did, he absolutely couldn't let go of the ring. He knew that much. He gripped the hard plastic and shoved it under his arms.

Then the world went black.

This had to be the strangest weather she'd ever experienced. Such volatile shifts certainly didn't happen where she came from. Chicago certainly had its share of windy days and dramatic dips in temperature from one day to the next, but nothing like this.

Elle promptly gathered all the children out of the ocean and then back onto the beach to the water sports cabana several feet away. No easy feat given her costume of the day. The chosen book today happened to be *The Little Mermaid*. As a result, she was clad in a shell-covered halter and a lengthy silicone fish tail with the narrowest slit at the bottom. Thanks to the storm, character-led story time had just been cut short.

With the seven toddlers under her care in tow, she led them to the shelter just in the nick of time. The lightning and thunder that immediately followed made her jump in her tail. More than a couple of the children began to sniffle in fear. She felt a gentle tug on one of her scales.

As best as the costume allowed, she crouched to a lower position so that she was at face level with the child, one she recognized as belonging to the American family who was staying at the resort.

Large, brown eyes full of anxiety met hers. "Miss Elle, is the lightning gonna hit us?"

Elle pulled the child closer and gave her a reassuring squeeze around her shoulders. "No, sweetie," Elle answered, making sure to keep her voice calm and steady. "As long as we stay put right here, we should be just fine."

The little girl gave her a skeptical look, clearly not convinced. The other children looked equally as apprehensive. Elle gave a silent prayer that the unexpected storm wouldn't last much longer. The children appeared ready to start crying at any moment. She could hardly blame them. One moment they were enjoying story time in the water, and the next they had found themselves in a scene straight out of a disaster film.

"Que es eso?" The question came from a small boy, spoken in his native Spanish. He thrust a pudgy, sand-covered finger in the direction of the water. Elle saw immediately what the little boy was referring to. She had to blink to make sure she was seeing it too.

What in the world?

In the distance, a few yards from the shoreline, an orange-and-white object was bobbing in the water. To her former high school lifeguard's eye, there was no mistaking what it was. Someone was in trouble out in the ocean, apparently floating on a safety rescue ring.

Elle glanced around in desperation. Aside from Señora Rita, the sweet little old lady who sold custom jewelry out of a kiosk on the beach, Elle and the kids were the only ones remaining in the immediate area. No one else was there to help the stranded swimmer. She didn't have her cell phone. There was nowhere to carry it in her shell-covered halter or her mermaid tail.

Elle's breath caught in her throat as a wave rose in front of the person floating in the water, blocking her view. Had he or she just gone under? A surge of relief ran through her when the person reappeared a second later. But it was tempered by the fact that there was still someone in trouble in the ocean.

"Is dat a person?" Chloe, the American child, asked.

"It certainly is." And what was she going to do about it? There hardly seemed to be much of a choice. She couldn't just leave the poor soul out there to drown. How would she ever live with herself?

Frantically, she began waving in Señora Rita's direction, several feet away. The woman was crouched under the roof of her kiosk, doing her best to stay dry. A futile attempt. The wind was blowing the rain in all manner of directions.

Finally, Señora Rita looked her way. Elle made the universal motion of "come here" by scooping her hand back and forth. The older woman appeared confused but finally stepped around the kiosk and began the perilous journey toward the cabana. It took so painfully long that Elle began to grow nauseous with concern for the stranded swimmer.

At last, Señora Rita made it into the cabana. The poor woman was soaking wet. In broken Spanish, Elle explained that she needed her to stay with the children for a few moments. Thank heavens Señora Rita seemed to understand and nodded her head.

Crouching again to the children's level, she

gave them all a serious glare. "I'm going to go try and help that person. I need you all to promise me that you'll stay right here with Señora Rita. Understood?"

She repeated it all in Spanish. Several tiny heads bobbed up and down seemingly in agreement. Still, not terribly reassuring. More than a couple of them looked confused and, heaven help her, more than a little anxious. But it would have to do. Elle didn't want to risk wasting any more time.

"I'll be back in no time," she reassured them, hoping fervently that it wasn't a lie. "Promise."

She was met with another round of nods that didn't do much to ease her discomfort. Again, she would have to believe that they understood. Bracing herself against the wind and rain, Elle hurried out of the small hut as best she could and made her way toward the water, discarding the cumbersome lower part of her costume along the way. Expertly, she dove into the waves. Childhood swim lessons and her several medal-winning years on the school dive team made the motions second nature. Nevertheless, her heart pounded in her chest with fear and doubt. Despite her one-year stint as a lifeguard at the country club pool, she'd never actually had to rescue anyone before.

The current was surprisingly strong. But

Elle hardly noticed, her sole focus on making it to the person in trouble out there. Keeping her strokes smooth and long, she opened her eyes long enough to locate her target. To her horror, they seemed to be drifting farther from the shoreline. Taking a deep breath, she ramped up her speed. Several agonizing moments later, she finally found herself within a few feet of the drifter.

Even with the terrible visibility, two things struck her at once. The person on the life ring was a man. One with ebony dark hair. Even with the slight tinge of purple shadowing his face, she could tell he was sporting a glowing tan.

Something tugged in the vicinity of her chest. A weird attraction that came out of nowhere and took her by surprise.

So not the time.

Focus!

Elle forced her attention back to the task at hand. Whoever he was, she'd reached him just in time. He seemed to be drifting in and out of consciousness. One moment, he appeared to be giving her a grateful smile, the next his eyes drew shut and his features grew slack.

Elle wrapped her arm around the rim of the rescue ring. Thrusting her legs as hard as she could, she did her best to propel them both toward the shore. Lord, it was strenuous work. He was heavier than she would have imagined. Between his weight and the strength of the oncoming waves, she had her work cut out for her. Luckily for both of them, she had well developed lungs given the years of swimming. Her parents and sisters often referred to her as a fish. If they could see her now.

Elle lost any sense of time as she made her way to the shore. Her chest was on fire and her limbs were on the verge of cramping. But she somehow managed to hang on and keep going.

By the time she finally reached the sand, every muscle in her body was screaming. Still, she wasted no time getting the man on his back and beginning chest compressions and alternately breathing into his mouth. One…two… three…

Please let him be okay.

Elle couldn't even be sure how much time had gone by before she felt a hand on her shoulder pushing her aside none too gently.

Help had finally arrived. A couple of EMTs began working on the stranger. Several agonizing seconds passed as she watched them resume what she'd begun. Finally, the man gave a wet sounding cough and began to heave. Moments later, he was loaded onto a stretcher and taken away.

Elle dropped to her bottom onto the sand, adrenaline still surging through her blood.

It took a while to get her breathing back to normal but when it finally did, she turned back to face the children and Señora Rita. Thank heavens, they all remained exactly where she'd left them, watching her with a combination of awe and horror. She hadn't even noticed until that moment that the storm had ended as quickly as it had begun. The sun shone bright once again in a clear and cloudless sky. As if none of it had happened.

"Well, look who's finally up and about."

Riko didn't bother to stifle a weary sigh as his brother approached him from the other side of the terrace. For a set of identical twins, they were different in as many ways as they were similar. Whereas Manny kept his dark hair straight with the use of two different products, Riko preferred his natural waves. Manny's style of dress was completely different also: he preferred casual shorts and T-shirts even in cool weather whereas Riko made sure he was dressed appropriately in the way the occasion called for.

Now, Manny was no doubt about to pepper him with the same questions about what had happened to him the other day. He appreciated everyone's concern, he really did.

But he was getting a little tired of the attention and the constant concern for his well-being. Mama in particular was bordering on obsessive, checking on him constantly, trying to pamper him like a toddler. It was bad enough she'd had the family physician move into Riko's personal wing in the palace. And everyone had so many questions, lobbed at him from every direction.

It wasn't as if he could remember the details clearly. Aside from a pair of haunting bluish-green eyes and fiery red hair in his mind's eye, he couldn't recall a thing about the accident. It was a blurry vision, dreamlike. A vision everyone assured him he must have imagined.

"How're ya feeling?" Manny asked, pulling out a metal wire chair and sitting across from him. A server immediately appeared with a steaming pot of coffee and a fresh mug.

"I'm fine," Riko answered. "No different than last night when you asked."

Manny grinned, taking a large swallow from his cup. "And we're gonna keep asking you until all of this becomes a distant memory." He set his beverage down. "Speaking of memory…"

Riko shook his head. "Nope, all I remember about the accident is what I already told you and everyone else."

Manny lifted an eyebrow. "Still sticking to that story, huh?"

"I know what I saw."

"Except you don't, big bro." Riko hated when Manny called him that. They were identical twins, for heaven's sake. Just because he happened to be delivered first hardly made him Manny's big bro.

His brother knew exactly how much it perturbed Riko to be referred to that way. Which was why Manny insisted on doing so.

"Somebody got me out of the water," Riko argued.

Manny nodded once. "Right. We've established that. The palace is trying to locate the person as we speak. The incredulous part is you seem to think your rescuer was a girl wearing seashells with fiery red hair. Who appeared out from the churning waves and swam you back to shore." His brother didn't bother to hide his disbelieving smirk.

"That's right."

Manny gave him a mischievous wink. "You sure you haven't been fantasizing about mermaids, big bro?"

Riko ignored the silly question. But it irked him enough that he wasn't going to let the nickname slide this time. Though he wasn't sure why he even bothered. Not like Manny would be deterred. "Don't call me that."

"You know I will."

Riko groaned out loud but decided to let it go. Again. "What's the latest about finding her?"

"Your mermaid?"

His brother could rile him like no one else on the planet. It was no wonder half the physical scars they both sported were a result of all their fisticuffs as children. The rest were mostly due to the two of them trying to outdo each other with reckless stunts like climbing the highest tree in the royal gardens or riding their bikes too fast downhill in the wooded area behind the palace.

"My rescuer," Riko corrected. "I'd like to make sure she's properly rewarded."

Manny's lips thinned, suddenly growing serious. "As would we all. Mama and Papa are very grateful."

Riko wasn't one to pass an opportunity to tease his brother, even about a matter this serious. "What about you, huh? Are you grateful that your twin brother didn't perish in a tumultuous sea? How badly would you have missed me?"

The mischievous grin immediately reappeared. "As if."

Riko leaned back in his chair, not ready to let his brother off the proverbial hook. "Huh. I seem to recall you arriving at my hospital bed before anyone else and looking rather concerned."

Manny shrugged. "I just knew Ramon and Tatyana would have been upset to lose their only uncle," he answered, referring to his six-year-old son and four-year-old daughter respectively. "I was concerned on their behalf."

"Right."

Manny rubbed his jaw with such exaggerated seriousness that Riko could tell without a doubt he was about to receive some more ridicule. "You know, it occurs to me that maybe we're looking for this person in the wrong places."

He knew better than to ask but couldn't seem to help himself. "How so?"

"Rather than on land, maybe we should be searching for her under the sea."

He'd been right. "Ha ha. Very funny. Don't you have a pregnant wife to tend to instead of sitting here hassling me?"

A shadow darkened his brother's eyes. Any hint of humor left his features. "What is it?" Riko asked, alarm churning in his gut.

Manny's lips tightened. "We didn't want to say anything so as not to worry anyone. Especially after…" He gestured in Riko's direction. "We swore the obstetrician to secrecy."

His alarm tripled. "Obstetrician? Is Isabel all right?"

Manny rubbed his forehead. "She's been experiencing some pain. Some other symptoms that aren't normal."

"You don't want to tell Mama?"

Manny shook his head. "We don't want to tell anyone." His brother didn't have to say aloud what they were both thinking. Riko was the exception. There'd never been any secrets between them. If it wasn't for his accident, Riko would have known that something wasn't sitting right with his brother.

Manny continued. "Not yet. Not until we know a little more. You know how Mama can get. Look at how she's reacting to your accident."

"Overreacting might be a better term. She needs to stop hovering." Riko took his brother's words as what they were, a desire to change the subject. When Manny was ready to talk more about his worry for his wife, Riko would be there to listen. He just hoped his sister-in-law didn't have anything serious to contend with during her pregnancy.

Manny was a strong man, but the love he had for his wife and children was definitely his soft spot. A weakness Riko understood but couldn't quite relate to himself.

He didn't know if he ever would.

CHAPTER TWO

ELLE WASN'T MUCH for cursing. But she was silently going through every expletive in her vocabulary as she collected her few belongings.

What in the world was she supposed to do now? As of an hour ago, she had no job, no place to stay, and very little money.

Of all the nerve. Diego had been looking for an excuse to get rid of her. And she'd handed him one on a silver platter by leaving the children with Señora Rita. Never mind that she'd done the only thing any sane person would have done in the same situation. What had Diego wanted her to do instead? Let the poor man drown?

Her phone buzzed on the wooden tableau across the room. No doubt her sister Lizzie calling. Again. She ignored it. As much as she loved her three sisters, she wasn't ready to talk to anyone in her family just yet about her latest disappointment. Though the word Mom and Dad would use would run more toward "failure."

Damn it. This last one was not her fault. The buzzing of her phone stopped finally. But it was immediately followed by several texts. Her sisters could be pretty demanding. One could hardly blame them. They didn't have time to waste trying to get hold of their younger sibling. They all had important careers and big responsibilities. Unlike her.

Striding over to the device to shut it off, Elle glanced at the screen.

Haven't heard from you in two days. If you don't call me back right away I'm sending the Spanish army after you.

Elle sighed. Being a prosecutor, her sister Lizzie saw her fair share of alarming crimes. As a result, she could be a bit overprotective. Annoyed but resigned, Elle plopped onto her stripped mattress and hit the call back button. She'd tell Lizzie just enough to get her off her back. For a while anyway. Her sister wouldn't relent until she knew the whole story.

And when she did, out of her misplaced concern, she would tell their parents. That was the last thing Elle needed.

Lizzie answered before the end of the first

ring. She didn't so much as bother with a "hello."
"Where have you been? Are you all right?"

Elle rubbed her forehead then mustered the
cheeriest voice she could. "I'm great. Everything's great. But I'm a little busy right now.
Can I call you back?"

She realized her mistake immediately. How
stupid of her. She'd overdone the enthusiasm.
Several seconds of silence passed before Lizzie
let loose. "Spill it, Arielle." Uh-oh, her sister was even using her full name. "What's the
matter?" she demanded to know. Elle tried to
hold strong, she really did. But the concern
and worry behind her sister's voice had her
undone in seconds.

She found herself blurting out the whole
story while utterly failing in her attempt not
to cry.

This was a disaster. Lizzie was going to go
straight to her parents. Then either Mom or
Dad, perhaps both, would be on the next flight
to Barcelona then onto a ferry straight to Majorca. She wouldn't even get a chance to try
and fix her predicament on her own. Never
mind that Elle had no idea how exactly she
would have done so. That was beside the point.

Surprisingly, Lizzie's next words had no
mention of notifying their parents. Instead,
her sister did some colorful swearing of her

own, outrage on Elle's behalf clear and strong in her voice. "Do you mean to tell me that SOB fired you for saving a man from drowning?"

"I'm afraid so," Elle answered. "He said I should have figured out a way to help the drowning man without leaving the kids with only a little old lady to watch over them."

"Wasn't that the guy who kept asking you out and you kept turning down?"

"One and the same," Elle answered, stifling another sob.

"Of all the… Clearly, he had ulterior motives."

Be that as it may, it still left Elle without a job or a roof over her head until she could think of a solution to her predicament.

"He's lucky I have no jurisdiction overseas," Lizzie added.

A hiccup escaped her throat. "Do you think he was right, Liz? Maybe even a little?" After all, she *had* left the children entrusted to Señora Rita's care. They hadn't been in any kind of danger, but what if one of them had wandered off and Señora Rita hadn't noticed?

"Absolutely not," her sister answered right away. "It was an impossible situation, and you used your best judgment. At the least, your creep of a boss could have given you a verbal warning or some other kind of slap on the wrist. Instead, he fires you."

The tension she hadn't even known she was holding in her center loosened. Up until she'd asked the question aloud, Elle hadn't even realized how much the notion that Diego might have been right had been bothering her. Her sister's reassurance had her feeling better, if only slightly.

"It's okay, Lizzie. I'll figure this out. Just promise me you won't tell Mom and Dad. I don't want them to worry." *Or worse, show up in Majorca*, she added silently.

Another long pause. Elle could practically see her sister debating internally about making such a promise.

"I'll come up with a plan. I just need some time," Elle pressed.

"Elle... I don't know. You don't even have a place to stay. Your room and board were a part of your employment at the resort."

A faint rustling sound from outside her door drew Elle's attention before she could answer. "I'll have to call you back, Lizzie. Just give me some time before you say anything to Mom and Dad."

She hung up the call before her sister could protest.

* * *

He could hear the distinct sound of someone crying behind the door. A child? No. It was a most definitely a woman. Riko paused mid-knock, unsure what to do. This was the correct resort and the correct room number. The palace guard had been very thorough in its investigation. He was here to personally express his gratitude to one Miss Arielle Stanton, American, originally from Chicago, Illinois, for having saved his hide from drowning two days ago. Not that he could remember it all that clearly.

Maybe this wasn't a good time.

Before he could make any kind of decision, the door was suddenly flung open. A startled pair of hazel-green eyes met his over the threshold. Eyes that turned instantly hostile. She looked him up and down then literally huffed before speaking. "If Diego sent you down to accompany me out of here, I assure you there's no need. I'm almost done packing."

Riko took a moment to process her words, trying to make some sense of them. Clearly, she'd mistaken him for someone else. Who was this Diego? A boyfriend perhaps? Had she been crying because of a recent breakup? The thought sent a wave of irritation over him, a feeling he couldn't identify. He was no doubt simply feeling protective of the woman after what she'd done for him the other day.

Though said woman was now shooting daggers at him.

Then she gave an exaggerated eye roll. "Look, I'll be out of here in no time. Tell Diego he didn't need to send a goon to try and intimidate me."

A goon? Intimidate her?

What kind of relationship had she been in anyway?

"I beg your pardon?" he asked for lack of anything else to say.

She began to shut the door. Reflexively, Riko stuck his foot out to stop her from closing it all the way. The action earned him a withering look. Somehow this interaction was escalating into some kind of strange confrontation.

"Who are you?" she demanded to know. "I haven't seen you on the grounds as part of the security detail."

Riko cleared his throat. "Señorita Stanton. Clearly, you have mistaken me for someone else. Allow me to introduce myself."

Her eyebrows furrowed with curiosity.

"My name is Eriko Rafael Suarez. I'm the man you rescued from nearly drowning the other day."

Her hand flew to her mouth. "Oh! I didn't recognize you! You're so…" She trailed off.

He nodded. "Yes, I imagine I looked quite different. For one, I'm a bit less unconscious now."

As far as jokes went, it was a rather bad one. Still, the corners of her mouth lifted ever so slightly. His attention fell to her lips, full and rose pink. Her hair was a shade of red he'd be hard-pressed to describe. Arielle Stanton was a looker by half. Riko didn't know what he'd been expecting, but he hadn't been prepared for the jolt of awareness coursing through his core that hadn't relented since she'd opened her door.

"Also, drier," she said. "You were much wetter when we first met."

He rubbed his chin. "Apologies. I should have thought to use a spray bottle on myself before approaching your door." Another terrible one. He so wasn't one to quip and joke with women he'd just met. What had gotten into him?

The slight smile turned to an all-out grin, and Riko wanted to pat himself on the back for putting it there. But it was short-lived. Any hint of humor suddenly left her eyes and the grin turned to a frown the next instant.

"So, I don't mean to be rude. But why are you here? This is not really a great time for me."

"I'm here to personally thank you. For myself and also on behalf of the king and queen."

She gave her head a shake. "The king and queen?"

"Of the kingdom of Versuvia. It's a small island nation a few nautical miles from Majorca to the east and the Spanish coast to the west. We're known as the Monaco of the Spanish world."

Her brows furrowed once more. Again, she eyed him up and down. "Right." She dragged out the word, pronouncing it as if it were three syllables. "Listen, I don't know how to break this to you, but I think you might have suffered some type of head injury during your accident. Probably wanna get that checked out." She began to shut the door again.

"Please wait. I know it might be hard to believe, but it's the truth. I'm Eriko Rafael Suarez, heir to the Versuvian throne. Firstborn son of King Guillermo and Queen Raina. My friends call me Riko." He tilted his head, waiting for her reaction.

She stuck her hand out. "Pleased to meet you. I'm Arielle Trina Stanton, the duchess of Schaumburgia. Daughter of King Alfred III and Queen Tammi, MD."

He simply stared at her, completely at a loss for words.

"See how that sounds?" she asked with a kind smile, humoring him apparently.

For the life of him, he couldn't figure out why he was still standing there. He'd felt obliged to thank her in person, and he'd done so. Anything else could be handled through his advisers. But something kept him planted in place where he stood, unable to walk away just yet.

So he decided to play along. "What a surprising coincidence, Your Highness." He performed an exaggerated bow slash curtsy.

The performance earned him a small chuckle. She crossed her arms in front of her chest. "Look, this has been entertaining and all. And I really am glad you're doing okay. But, like I said, I'm kind of in the middle of something. Packing up my apartment that I have to leave. And besides, I've run out of the Earl Grey I usually serve to other royalty."

Definitely his cue to depart. So why exactly did he say what he did next? "Perhaps I can buy you a cup then? If you can step away from your current task. I can even send a couple of men who are waiting outside to finish your packing for you."

Her jaw fell. "Wow. That's some real commitment to the bit. You're really still going with whole prince thing, huh?"

"I don't really have a choice. Birthright being what it is and all. I'll wait here in the hall while you go google me."

He should probably have just led with that option. Not that he hadn't enjoyed the little exchange.

She threw up her hands. "Fine. I'll go do that. If it means I can get on with my day. Versuvia, you said?"

"Yes."

She shut the door before he could thank her for obliging. What a fun errand this had turned out to be. He happened to have a morning meeting on the island with the mayor. Figured he'd take care of this as well. He'd only planned on introducing himself, handing her his card and directing her to call the palace with anything she might want or need as a gesture of gratitude. Instead, here he stood waiting for her do some basic research to confirm he was who he said he was.

The look on her face when she opened the door several minutes later made it all more than worthwhile. Her jaw agape, eyes wide, shaking her head in disbelief.

"Holy sh—" She cupped her hand to her

mouth. "Oh! I probably shouldn't swear in front of royalty, huh?"

Joining him in the hall, she began to pace a few feet then back to where he stood. "Wow. Do you mean to tell me that the man I pulled out of the water was a real life, verified, true-blood son of a king and queen?"

"Firstborn. Although, that's something of a fluke. I only beat my twin brother by a matter of minutes."

She stared at him, still stunned. "Where's your entourage? How are you here by yourself?"

He pointed up. "They're waiting for me upstairs in the lobby and along the street. Figured you'd be less startled if I showed up alone rather that with two bodyguards and my personal secretary."

"Huh. Well, consider me startled nevertheless. Wait till the girls hear about this."

"Girls?"

"My sisters. They're not going to believe any of this. I can hardly believe it myself. An honest to goodness prince, here at my door. A prince I dragged ashore."

She really was delightful.

"So about that tea. Or coffee if you prefer?"

Her eyebrows lifted. "Give me a second to

grab my bag. What kind of fool woman would turn that offer down?"

Riko chuckled and watched as she reached for a large leather bag hanging off a hook on the wall.

His afternoon had just gotten exponentially more interesting.

This couldn't really be happening. She had to be in the middle of some kind of prank someone was pulling. Elle looked around for any hidden cameras as she followed the man— rather, the prince—upstairs. Maybe she was in the middle of some kind of dream, and she should pinch herself to see if it would wake her. Or she wanted to pinch the man standing next to her in the elevator as they rode up to the lobby floor.

A prince!

How in the world had a prince almost drowned until she'd swum out to get him? Only one of the many burning questions she was yearning to ask. It was why she'd agreed to grab a cup of tea with him, despite all she had to do.

Diego could wait for her apartment key. Right now, she had a much more pressing engagement. To think, she'd almost sent him away this morning. Thank goodness he'd persevered, despite her trying to slam the door in his face.

Now, she watched as he spoke into the smart watch at his wrist in rapid-fire Spanish. Too fast for her to understand.

He clicked off the device then turned to her. "I've asked that arrangements be made to be able to leave the building while drawing as little attention to us as possible. And that a private room be secured for us in the back area of a nearby café."

That seemed like an awful lot of trouble for a measly cup of caffeine. But what did she know? She wasn't of royal blood like her companion here.

"Sounds like a lot of hassle."

He shrugged. "I'm used to it. I don't get recognized that often in Majorca, but it does happen occasionally."

When they reached the lobby doors, a big burly man in a dark suit opened the glass door for them. "It's clear to enter the vehicle, Your Highness."

"*Gracias*, Juan," Riko answered the man, guiding her to a black SUV parked a few feet away, his hand at the small of her back. A puddle of warmth resonated through her where his palm touched.

Just haven't been touched in a while, that's

all. And definitely never been touched by a prince.

By the time they'd arrived at the café and were led to a back room, reality still hadn't quite settled in her mind. It had to be one of her earlier theories—dream or prank. She wasn't really sitting down in a chair a real prince had just pulled out for her.

A server appeared immediately with a large tray of pastries and fruit. Another immediately followed him with two steaming carafes of a heavenly scented coffee that filled the air. They hadn't even had to order anything.

"You seem deep in thought," he said, shrugging the jacket off his shoulders to reveal a crisp white shirt over a toned chest and arms. Elle forced herself to avert her gaze from his physique and look straight into his eyes instead. They were an unusual shade of brownish black that a girl could easily get lost in. The man certainly had a lot going for him.

"You have to know I have a lot of questions," she began as the man poured their beverages then left without a word.

"What do you Americans say…? Shoot them my way."

She nodded. "Close enough. First of all, what should I even call you? Like, Your Highness, or something?"

He chuckled softly, took a sip of his drink. "Well, seeing as I owe you such a big debt, I consider us to be something akin to friends."

Right. She wasn't naive enough to believe that was a real possibility. This wasn't her first experience with a celebrity of sorts. She'd sung backup on tour last summer with the latest social media sensation turned pop star. But this experience was something else entirely.

"So, call me Riko like my other friends do," he continued.

That suggestion didn't quite sit right with her. Was it really okay to be so informal with him? Enough to call him by his first name?

"What else?" he prompted.

Elle cleared her throat. "I'm not quite sure where to begin."

"How about I start then? With my own questions."

"You have questions about me?" Elle didn't trust herself to pick up her cup, her hands were shaking with nervous excitement. She knew he was just being polite. Why would a royal have any curiosity about someone like her?

"Certainly. What do you do when you're not saving strangers from a watery death?" he asked.

"Believe it or not, you are my first and only rescue."

"You do realize you didn't actually answer my question."

Elle gave her head a shake. She couldn't recall what he'd asked her. Her mind didn't seem to want to work around this man. "I'm sorry. What was it again?"

Riko chuckled. Somehow, he grew even more handsome every time he laughed. She could really see herself getting used to being around this man.

Like there was any chance of that happening. She had to remember she was only sitting here through a series of very random circumstances.

"How about you just tell me what you're doing here in Majorca?"

Elle ducked her head, embarrassed. It had been hard enough explaining her journey to the Spanish island to her parents and siblings. It would be mortifying explaining it to someone like him.

"I see it's something of a sore spot then," Riko said when she didn't answer for several beats.

Oh, what the hell? She might as well tell him the whole sordid story. Not like she would ever see him again after today. "I was chosen to perform in a traveling vocal band. We were touring Europe. Had just landed for the latest gig in Barcelona."

"You're a singer."

She could only nod. Elle couldn't even justify calling herself that anymore. "We were playing some small venues when the whole thing fell apart."

And once more, she'd found herself without a job or any kind of money. Only this time, she was thousands of miles from home in a foreign country.

"What happened?" Riko asked.

Elle released a deep breath. "Everything came apart when the bassist found the drummer in bed with the keyboardist. Who happened to be his wife."

Riko merely lifted an eyebrow, so she continued. "Anyway, the bassist took pity on me seeing as I was so far from home and recommended me for an entertainer position here at one of the resorts." The woman had neglected to mention that the opening was for a children's entertainer. Basically, a babysitter in costume. Not that it would have mattered; she hadn't exactly been in a position to turn the job down.

The job she no longer even had.

"When are you onstage next?"

Elle huffed out a laugh. "They never had me

onstage. Basically I was there to entertain the kids while their parents enjoyed their vacation."

Riko rubbed his chin. "I see."

She reached for a sugary churro, drizzled in chocolate glaze. "It hardly matters now anyway," she continued, not quite certain why she kept going. It made no sense that she was comfortable sharing so much with this man she'd just met.

"Why's that?" he asked.

"Because I managed to get myself fired. Which means I also need to find a place to stay."

His eyes narrowed with concern and question.

"The room came with the job," she explained, taking a bite of the pastry. It melted in her mouth like some kind of sweet, buttery cloud. It was hard not to groan out loud.

"Maybe I can make a phone call to this boss of yours. Ask him to rethink his decision."

Elle immediately shook her head. "That's very nice of you. But, no thanks. I don't think I want to work for Diego any longer anyway."

"Why were you let go?"

Elle did her best to explain. She didn't want Riko to think she faulted him in any way.

Riko listened intently and silently while she did her best to summarize the events that had led to her pulling him semiconscious out of the water.

She was nearly breathless by the time she finished, finally adding, "I only left the children with Señora Rita for a few short minutes. And they were totally fine."

"So you're saying I'm the reason you're now unemployed. The least I can do is offer you some type of financial gift. Especially given that I'm the cause of your current predicament."

She shook her head once again. "No. I refuse to take your charity for doing what any decent person would have done under the same circumstances. Besides, Diego's been looking for a reason to fire me for weeks now. It was bound to happen sooner or later."

"This wouldn't be charity, Elle. Consider it a reward for your efforts."

"It would still feel like charity to me."

He looked ready to argue, but something in her expression must have made him think better of it.

He leaned back in his chair, rubbed a palm down his face. He studied her for several long moments before saying, "Well, if you don't want me to intervene on your behalf with this Diego, and you refuse to accept any kind of reward, I might have one last idea."

That sounded encouraging. "I'm all ears."

"I don't understand that phrase in the least."

"It's an American idiom. It means I'm open to suggestions. What did you have in mind?"

"Perhaps there's someone else I can call on your behalf."

"So let me get this straight, you want us to hire a nanny who was just let go because she was bad at watching kids?" His brother sounded amused more than annoyed over the phone.

Riko glanced through the doorway where Elle still sat at the small wooden table, sipping her third cup of coffee. "Yes, I know how it sounds. But I explained why she left the children. And they weren't even unattended. We owe her."

"Riko, you told me she was fired."

"That wasn't her fault. She was fired on account of me."

"Why can't you just pay her?"

Riko pinched the bridge of his nose. "I tried that. She refuses. Says it would be accepting our charity."

"So she asked you for a job?"

Riko stepped farther into the hallway, toward the kitchen. "No, in fact, she has no idea I'm doing this. But it's perfect, isn't it? You and Isabel need a nanny while she's on bed rest. And Elle has experience taking care of children."

"I suppose it would be nice to be able to stop searching so that Isabel can focus on healing. The last woman the agency sent was completely unacceptable."

Riko pounced on his brother's hesitation. "Come on, Manny. I feel like I owe it to this woman to help her fix what I had a hand in breaking. Maybe we can just give it a trial run, see how she does. You can keep looking for a permanent replacement in the meantime."

He could hear his brother's long sigh from across several miles of sea. "Let me run it by Isabel. But I warn you, she will have the final say, big bro."

"Fair enough."

Elle greeted him with a shy smile when he reentered the room. "I'm guessing you called a contact at another resort to see about openings."

"Something like that," he answered, pulling out his chair and taking his seat again.

"You didn't need to do that, Your Hi…uh, Riko. But thank you. It's very kind of you."

He waved that away. "Would you like anything else to eat or drink?"

"No, actually I should be getting back. Finish packing." Lifting her cloth napkin off her lap, she dabbed it at the corners of her mouth.

Riko had to look away. It was bad enough when she'd taken a bite of churro and gotten some of the glaze on her bottom lip. For an insane moment, he'd envisioned himself helping her remove that glaze in all sorts of ways.

Focus.

She started to stand, and Riko felt a surge of sadness. They'd been sitting here for close to two hours. He had things to do, calls to make back at the hotel. Yet he found he didn't want the time to end. He couldn't recall the last time he'd felt that way about time spent with a woman. It didn't help that any woman he'd been with in the past had been handpicked as his date.

"What about after that? Where will you go?"

A shadow crossed her face. "I can find a hostel or something. There has to be an opening somewhere that isn't exorbitantly expensive."

Riko stood as well, shrugged back into his jacket. There was no lodging in this resort town that wasn't exorbitantly expensive. Especially if needed last minute.

He had no intention of letting her find that out the hard way.

She couldn't have heard him right. "I beg your pardon?" Elle asked with a shake of her head.

Had Riku really just asked her to spend the night with him?

A surge of anger burned in her chest. Along with a stinging disappointment. She should have known he seemed too good to be true.

He held a hand up. "I can tell you're getting the wrong idea. I assure you it's not what you think."

"I certainly hope not. Because I could have sworn you just made me an offer to spend the night with you at your hotel."

He nodded once. "I did. Technically."

What on earth did that mean? "Technically?"

"I'm staying at the Hotel Galencia. The suite I'm in has two separate bedrooms. It's the same suite they book for me whenever I'm in town. The second room always sits empty. There's no reason it should tonight."

Well, that sounded much more reasonable than what she'd been thinking. A rush of heat flamed her cheeks. She'd insinuated that he'd been coming on to her with a sketchy proposition. How mortifying. As if someone in his position would have any interest in her that way.

Embarrassment aside, did she dare take him up on his offer? She didn't know the man from Adam. "I don't know…"

"If it makes a difference, each door has a lock."

That certainly helped matters. But still. A girl couldn't be too careful.

She supposed it wouldn't hurt to take a look at the place. Not like she had a lot of options to go with here.

An hour later, Elle stepped out of the marble shower stall and glanced at her image in the three-panel mirror on the opposite wall. That had to be the most luxurious bathing she'd ever done. A girl could get used to such plush surroundings.

The suite beat any hostel that might have been her shelter tonight. Elle would have had to use a shared bathroom with only cold, rusty water running through crumbling faucets. Riko's offer had been heaven-sent. All the while, he was also scouting a job for her.

Her phone buzzed on her mattress in the other room. Probably her sister calling for an update. Elle adjusted the thick Turkish towel wrapped around her and made her way slowly to the other room. Her muscles felt loose and languid for the first time in as long as she could remember. Amazing what a strong jet of hot water could do for a person.

The text message on her phone screen was

indeed from her sister. Elle's stomach tightened as she read it.

Dad is about to videoconference you. I strongly suggest you answer.

So much for the relaxation the hot shower had afforded. Her shoulders tensed tightly, and she felt the beginnings of a tension headache. Conversations with her father always ramped up her anxiety.

Sure enough, her screen lit up with her father's photo and the icon for an incoming video call. For just a split second, Elle was tempted to ignore it. After all, she could have still been in the shower. But that would just be putting off the inevitable. Her father would simply call back until she answered, and the delay would only serve to make him irate.

Too late. When she clicked to accept the call, it was clear as day that her father was already irate. To make matters worse, he appeared to be in full power attorney mode—his silver-gray hair perfectly coifed, dark navy tie around his neck, collar stiff and straight.

"Hi, Dad."

"Elle, how are you?" He didn't give her a chance to answer. "What's this about you being unemployed?"

How in the world did he know? If Lizzie had told him about her predicament, she was going to throttle her sister as soon as she saw her again. But Elle tossed that assumption aside as soon as it had hit. That didn't sound like Lizzie at all. Her sister had promised.

"Just a temporary setback, Dad. I already have other prospects lined up. But how…?"

"Your former employer called the house. To see if this address was where to send your final paperwork."

Diego strikes again.

"He said you'd neglected your duties."

"That's not what—"

But he cut her off again.

"Are you finally ready to stop gallivanting around the world and come back home?"

"I'm not exactly gallivanting, Dad. I was here on tour," she said, telling him what he already knew but refused to acknowledge.

Her father waved his hand in dismissal. "Just come back. We'll have you reenrolled in your studies in no time."

Elle gripped the phone tightly in her hand. She really didn't have the energy for this same old argument. Simply didn't have it in her. So she remained silent, pacing and nodding until her father was finally done. It took much too long.

"I'll think about it, Dad," she lied when he'd finally finished his rant.

"See that you do." With that, her screen went dark.

The sound of someone clearing their throat behind her startled Elle into dropping her phone. "Oh!"

With no small amount of mortification, Elle realized she'd paced herself right out of her room and into the common lounge area. Riko stood a few feet away by the wet bar, a glass tumbler in his hand. Even at this time of night, he looked like something out of a cologne ad. Polished and handsome and definitely prince material. He'd unbuttoned the top three buttons of his shirt, rolled his sleeves up to the elbow. And here she stood in nothing but a towel, her wet hair a messy nest atop her head.

"You heard all that, huh?"

He nodded once. "Sounded intense."

She rubbed her forehead. "My father is nothing if not intense."

"Want to talk about it?"

"Not particularly." What she wanted was to somehow forget that her father considered her to be flaky and impulsive, with no direction in life.

Riko nodded once and took a sip of his drink. "Well, if it helps, I heard back about the job proposal I had in mind for you. It's a go. You got the job. If you want it." He lifted his glass to her in a mini salute.

Elle had to bite down on her urge to squeal in delight. Finally, some good news. "Thank you! Will I be working at another resort?"

"Not quite. You'll actually be working at the castle. For the royal family."

CHAPTER THREE

Three days later

"Ms. STANTON. On behalf of the royal family, please allow me to welcome you to Versuvia."

Elle walked down the steps of the prop plane and approached the middle-aged smiling gentleman who waited on the tarmac to greet her. A sleek black sedan with shiny silver tire rims idled behind them, the windows tinted dark gray. She glanced around, a tinge of disappointment in the pit of her stomach. What had she expected? That the crown prince himself would be there waiting for her? How silly to think someone that important would run such a common errand. Besides, he'd done more than enough for her already. Plenty in fact.

"I'm Phillipe, Prince Eriko's steward," the man announced, taking her carry-on from her and extending his hand. Silver-haired, tan and wearing a pinstriped gray suit, he looked straight out of central casting for the role of royal assistant.

Elle swallowed a nervous lump in her throat and smoothed the skirt of her muslin dress. Perhaps she should have taken more care with her appearance. She was dressed pretty casually, in a summery sleeveless dress and flat leather sandals. Her chaperone appeared as if he was about to attend a state dinner.

She took the hand he offered and followed him to the vehicle. The driver's window rolled down slowly, and a hatted, mustached younger man gave her a friendly smile and slight nod of greeting before rolling the glass back up.

Phillipe helped her into the car and soon they were driving down the runway, eventually turning onto a lined paved street.

"How was your flight, Ms. Stanton?"

Elle cleared her throat. She fervently hoped this level of formality wasn't going to be the norm during her tenure here. Phillipe and the driver seemed friendly enough, but there was no mistaking the all-business atmosphere.

"Quite lovely, thank you. Ri—" She stopped before completing the word. Even if Riko had explicitly told her over coffee few days ago that she should use his first name, somehow it felt inappropriate under the circumstances. Clearing her throat, she began again. "His Highness was very generous to have arranged the flight for me."

Generous was hardly a sufficient word. He'd given her three extra days' stay in his suite so that she could get her affairs in order and enjoy a little rest.

She'd spent those days on a cloud of relief. Before he'd knocked on her door, she'd had no idea what her future was going to hold. Riko had presented her with a dream job—working in a palace with good pay and an elegant roof over her head. But now, as she sat in the back of a late model SUV in a plush leather seat with a tuxedoed driver and someone who called himself the prince's steward, a blossom of anxiety spread in her chest and spread lower to her stomach.

What exactly had she gotten herself into?

Riko had no doubt his personal secretary was fed up. He could hardly blame the man. This had to be at least the fourth time he'd had to repeat himself. Riko couldn't recall the last time he'd been this distracted.

Once more, he forced his mind to focus on the numbers before him on the spreadsheet the other man was referring to—something about a discrepancy in reports about an upcoming change to the euro exchange rate and the effect it might have on the kingdom's many casinos.

Had she arrived at the palace yet?

There he went again. Riko puffed out a breath of frustration and flung his handcrafted gold pen on the top of his mahogany desk. The action earned a small gasp of surprise from his exasperated assistant.

"I'm sorry, Marco," he said, running his hand down his face. "I'm a bit out of sorts this morning. Perhaps we can resume this meeting later in the afternoon."

The truth was he'd been out of sorts since he'd left Majorca three days ago. His mind replayed the events of the afternoon repeatedly. His café date with Elle had felt like a breath of fresh air.

Marco didn't need to be told twice. He immediately stood and snapped the cover of his tablet closed. "Of course, sir. Ring me whenever you're ready." In no small amount of haste, he strode to the door and shut it behind him.

Riko stood and paced over to the large bay window across the room. For the first time he could recall, he regretted the fact that his office faced the back gardens and not the mountain road that led to the main entrance of the castle. Usually he loved to be able to gaze out at this view, the myriad colors, the lush greenery of the expertly manicured shrubbery.

Today, he wished he were watching the road instead.

There was nothing for it. Without giving himself time to think any longer, he made his way out of his office and down the circular stairway to the first floor to see if she was here yet.

He might not fully remember the afternoon of the boat accident, but thoughts of Elle Stanton seemed to occupy his mind without end.

Elle wasn't sure what she'd been expecting. But she certainly hadn't been prepared for the breathtaking view that met her as they drove through a tall, automated metal gate and up a circular road meandering around a high stony mountain. Before long, a majestic castle appeared in the distance like something out of a fairy tale movie. Her breath caught in her throat at the scene before her as the car drew closer.

With red stone walls and two towers that reached the clouds, the structure was framed by the ocean on one side and an emerald green field on the other. She still hadn't quite recovered from her awestruck reaction by the time the car came to a stop in front of a grand brick stairwell that led up to a massive pair of wooden doors. A uniformed footman appeared out of nowhere and immediately opened the car door for her. Phillipe spoke to him in Spanish, and he gave a quick nod then made for the doors.

"This way please, Ms. Stanton," Phillipe said, then took her arm and led her up the steps. The doors seemed to magically open on their own, and Elle found herself stepping into a foyer that reminded her of the Art Institute of Chicago, the city's historical art museum. Marble tile floors, high arched ceiling and ionic columns on either side of a wide circular staircase. A chandelier the size of a small car hung glittering high above her head.

No doubt about it, she'd entered an honest to goodness castle.

"I'll show you to your room to give you a chance to freshen up," Phillipe told her, his voice echoing slightly off the massive walls.

"If you would follow me," he added. If he had any indication of just how awestruck Elle was, he showed no sign of it. Though she was certain her wonderment had to be written all over her face. She'd never seen such a magnificent structure in her life, let alone been inside one. To think, she'd be living here. A week ago what she'd been referring to as home was a dark, six by six foot room in the basement of a hotel with one solitary light bulb hanging from the ceiling as her only source of light.

Phillipe cleared his throat, looking at her expectantly. That's right. He'd asked her to follow him. Fully expecting to be led up the staircase, she was surprised when he led her around the sculpted banister instead and through a wide hallway behind the steps. He stopped at a glass panel and pressed a button. The wall slid open to one side to reveal a steel door elevator. He motioned for her to step in then joined her inside. A moment later, the doors opened once more to reveal a wide corridor.

"These are the staff quarters," Phillipe explained, removing a key from his jacket pocket as he led her to a wooden door several feet away. He unlocked it then handed her the key. "This is your personal room, miss. Though I'm certain you will also have lodging in the Granada wing."

She blinked at him. "The Granada wing?"

He nodded. "Where Prince Manuel and Princess Isabel reside with their children."

Right! Her employers. Thanks to them, and Riko, she'd gone from barely having a place of her own to being able to claim two rooms in a castle.

"Maribel, our lead housekeeper," Phillipe

continued, "will be by in a few moments to give you a tour and present you with a preliminary schedule." He executed a small bow that Elle mimicked though she had no idea if that was the right protocol. She really was out of her element here. A true fish out of water.

"If you'll excuse me." With that, the man turned and left the room.

Elle clasped a hand to her chest as soon as he was gone. A sliding screen door led to a balcony that overlooked the ocean. The furniture in the room appeared handcrafted and expensive. Again, the feelings of inadequacy she'd managed to brush off during the ride here began to resurface.

Suddenly, she felt completely disoriented and alone. She was in a strange land, where she didn't even really know the language. The resort where she'd worked less than a week ago drew guests and employees from all over the world.

She'd been merely one more visitor there among many. Here, she was a complete outsider. So far, there'd been no sign of the prince who'd invited her here. Now that she thought about it, it had been beyond foolish of her to think that she might have any kind of interaction with him.

No matter. Prince Eriko Rafael Suarez was

not the reason she was here. She was here to do a job and nothing more. The sooner she got that into her head, the better off she'd be and the sooner she'd be able to adjust to her new surroundings.

Or so she told herself.

Before she could do any more wallowing, a gentle knock sounded on her door. That must be Maribel, here to show her around. Not a moment too soon.

"Come in."

Elle's breath caught in her throat as the door opened. Then she sighed in relief. Riko had shown up to welcome her, after all.

But her smile froze before it could fully form on her face as she instantly realized her mistake. The gentleman standing before her might have had the same friendly smile and the very same facial features of the man she'd pulled out of the water that day, but there was no question it wasn't him.

Elle's heart sank, but she forced the smile she no longer felt. This had to be Prince Manuel. Riko's twin brother, the man she'd be working for.

The one who had really hired her.

"This is the second time I've seen you in this hallway, big bro. Why don't you just go ahead and ask where she is?" Manny asked with no small amount of glee as Riko rounded the corner and nearly barreled into him.

He adjusted the collar of his shirt and tried to look clueless before he answered. "I have no idea what you might be referring to. I was just on my way to find Marco in order to resume our meeting that was unexpectedly delayed this morning." Never mind that he'd been the reason for that delay.

Manny gave him a knowingly suspicious smile. "Honestly, I have no idea why you bother trying to lie to me. After all these years, you have to know it never works."

Riko shrugged. "It's always worth a try."

"Save it, man. Maribel is taking her around the gardens until Isabel is up to seeing anyone for the day. I already introduced myself. I take it you'd like to find her."

"Fine. You're right," Riko admitted. "Just trying to be polite and cordial." It was the truth. Riko was merely being courteous. It was only polite to welcome Elle to the castle on her first day. He had been the one to hire her, after all. His intentions were completely innocent and honorable. The small voice in his head that wanted to argue that point could easily be ignored. For now.

Riko stepped around his brother to make his

way to the back door leading to the royal gardens, but Manny stopped him before he'd gone more than a couple of steps. "Funny thing is," his brother began, "I have no doubt she thought I was you at first."

"That's hardly novel, it happens all the time."

"Sure it does. But you should have seen the look of disappointment on her face when she realized it was me and not you at her door."

Riko decided to ignore that as he resumed his path, as well as the clear tone of mischief in Manny's voice. Though it was much harder to ignore the electricity buzzing along his skin at his brother's words.

...the look of disappointment on her face...

Warmth curled in his core at the thought before he shrugged it off. His brother was probably exaggerating about Elle's disappointment at finding Manny at her door instead of himself. An attempt to try to goad Riko into some kind of response, to see if he reacted at the possibility that Elle might be excited to see him.

Luckily, Riko had managed not to take the bait.

It took him a good ten minutes to find them, the Suarez royal garden being one of the most immaculate and extensive this side of Europe. She stood next to their lead housekeeper, listening with her head tilted to whatever the older woman was telling her. Even with her back turned to him, there was no mistaking the thick, long braid of fiery red hair. An insane image of undoing that braid and letting the thick waves of hair flow through his fingers ran through his mind before he forcibly pushed it out.

Riko felt his pulse quicken as he approached. How utterly silly of him to feel such excitement to see her again. It had only been three days, for heaven's sake. What in the world was wrong with him? He almost turned around before the two women could notice he was there. Which only led to more self-disdain. He was the crown prince of Versuvia. He wasn't supposed to turn tail and run from any woman.

"The children particularly like to picnic in this spot," Maribel was explaining, gesturing to the wooden table and matching child-sized chairs. "They often take their lunches here."

Elle bobbed her head up and down in an enthusiastic nod, then seemed to take a quick note on her phone. It appeared Ms. Stanton was taking her nanny duties seriously already.

Suddenly, Elle's shoulders stiffened and her fingers paused in the act of clicking on her phone screen, as if she'd sensed his presence. She turned to face him slowly when he was just a few feet away. The smile that spread over her face when her eyes met his had his steps faltering.

"I can take it from here, Maribel," Riko said once he'd reached them.

The woman's eyes grew wide at the suggestion. "Are you certain, sir?"

Riko made a show of glancing at his watch. "Most certainly. I could use the fresh air, and I find myself between appointments." He added the latter lie with an almost bored tone to try to sound a bit more convincing.

Maribel glanced between the two of them, still clearly confused. A beat passed before she spoke. "Very well, then. Thank you. I'll go check on dinner." She gave him a single nod and bid Elle goodbye.

An awkward moment passed between them once they were alone. Then they both spoke at once, only serving to add to the awkwardness.

"How was your trip here?" Riko asked just as Elle began thanking him again.

Her laughter at the clumsy exchange served to break the ice, dissolving the discomfort. Suddenly, they were the same people who'd shared coffee and pastries at a small café in Majorca a few days ago.

"I met your brother earlier," Elle said as they began walking along the perimeter of the grassy knoll the two ladies had been standing on. "The resemblance is uncanny," she added.

He let out a huff of a chuckle. "Yes, we get that a lot."

"I'm looking forward to meeting the children when they get back. And Princess Isabel when she's up for it."

"I'm sure they will all be delighted to meet you as well. As will my mother and father."

Elle paused for a moment.

"What is it?" Riko asked. She'd gone several shades paler, her eyes wide.

Then it occurred to him. Of course, she was nervous about meeting his mother and father. More accurately, she was nervous about meeting the king and queen.

He leaned in closer to her. "Relax. They don't bite."

Elle's delight at finally seeing Riko was quickly replaced by trepidation at his words. Maybe it had been foolish of her, but she hadn't actually considered that the king and queen would bother meeting an inconsequential nanny in their son's employ. Though she supposed it made sense. What little she'd seen of this family so far told her they were a tight-knit and close one, royal titles notwithstanding. Of course such people would want to meet the person who'd be looking after their precious grandchildren. She should have thought to better prepare herself mentally for this whole experience.

But then Riko leaned over to whisper something flippant about his parents not biting her, and she could hardly think at all. For a time back in Majorca after he'd left, she'd fancied that she'd imagined how handsome he was, how charming. That maybe her mind had embellished his attributes. Seeing him in the flesh again eradicated any such notion. If anything, he was even more strikingly good-looking. His dark hair glistened in the bright sun, the masculine scent of him reached her nose over the gentle breeze to mix with the salt air of the sea. He'd started growing a beard, which lent a hint of ruggedness to his features. A tingle ran through her hands at the thought of running her fingers over his chin to feel the stubble there. She took a step back before she succumbed to the urge and did something ridiculously silly.

"I probably should have warned you about my brother," Riko said as they resumed walking. "He can be a bit of a personality."

She let out a small laugh. "On the contrary. I thought he was quite charming."

Riko gave her a small eye roll. "That's Manny

all right. Most people, particularly the ladies, and quite a few men, come to think of it, find him charming. Always been that way." His lips tightened as he said the words, but Elle sensed no malice or negativity behind them.

"You're something of a charmer yourself," she said, surprising herself with her candor. Then figured she may as well go all in and continue. "In fact, one might even call you Prince Charming."

He flashed her a playful smile. "Hardly. Besides, if we're going to discuss fairy tales, I'd say our initial watery meeting is more in line with the story of a different prince, is it not?"

A bubble of laughter rose from deep within her chest. How right he was.

They'd come upon a wall of shrubbery several feet tall, trimmed with precise edges. Riko took her gently by the shoulders. "Come here. I want to show you something."

He led her several feet down the wall until they reached an opening several feet wide.

"It's a maze," he explained, gesturing her inside. "There's a stone water fountain in the center. Think you can find it?"

Elle was delighted at the prospect. But she'd never been very good at puzzles. "I don't have much of a sense of direction," she admitted.

"I'll be right behind you if appear to be getting too lost."

"Then I guess I have nothing to lose by trying."

"That's the spirit."

Bolstered by his encouragement, she dove in and tried several different paths with Riko fast on her heels. It didn't take long before Elle was ready to call it quits. Just when she thought she heard the trickling of the water fountain loud and clear, she took what she thought was the right turn only to have the noise grow fainter.

Throwing her hands up, she turned on her heel to concede defeat. Only she'd completely misjudged how close Riko was behind her.

"Umph!" She'd barreled right into his chest.

A pair of strong, steady arms immediately reached around her to hold her steady. Time seemed to stop as neither one of them moved so much as an inch.

They were completely alone, surrounded by greenery. The shrubs around them tall and isolating. As if they were the only two people in the world. The warmth of his breath against her cheek sent a flame through her middle.

Elle couldn't help but shift her gaze to his mouth, hovering so close to hers.

Heaven help her, he was lowering his head, his arms around her waist tightening ever so slightly but just enough to make her head feel light and woozy.

Something flickered behind his eyes and then a curtain suddenly seemed to fall behind their depths. He pulled his head back, away from hers. Whatever had just happened, the moment was over. Elle couldn't decide whether to feel relieved or rife with disappointment.

Finally, some semblance of sanity crawled back into her brain and made her pull away and step out of his arms. With shaky hands, she smoothed her hair out of her face.

Riko's expression was impossible to decipher. Shadows fell over his features, his eyes remained dark and unreadable.

"I should probably head back to the castle," she said, finally managing to get her mouth to work. "I imagine the children are back by now. Wouldn't want to appear to be slacking on my first day."

Riko's lips tightened just before he took a step back also. Despite the small space between them, she suddenly felt as if it might as well have been a chasm miles wide.

What had just happened?

"I suppose you're right," he said. "We'll save the fountain search for some other time."

Not any time soon, Elle thought as she followed him down the path and out of the maze.

Given the way her heart still pounded in her chest as they stepped into the grassy clearing, one thing was certain—being alone with Riko in such a secluded, private way again would be nothing short of foolish.

She was here to do a job until she could figure out what the future had in store for her. The last thing she needed was to lose her heart along the way.

Riko slammed the door of his study shut and began pacing around his desk. What in the world had he been doing?

Silly question. The answer was clear, wasn't it?

He'd behaved like a hormonal teenager with a woman in his family's employ. For heaven's sake, he'd almost kissed her back there. How inappropriate. He was the heir to the throne. He needed to maintain decorum at all times, behave in a manner fitting his station. Coming on to the family's new nanny definitely fell outside such parameters.

Nothing like that could ever happen again. He had to make sure of it. He had nothing to offer Arielle Stanton. His future was laid out for him by centuries of precedent. There were expectations he would need to fulfill as the future king.

His phone vibrated on his desk with a message, pulling him out of his mental rant. When he glanced at it, he could only shake his head. The irony was almost comical. Like a reminder from the universe, the message from his father served to emphasize exactly what he'd just been thinking.

Please see me in my quarters within the hour. Infanta Gina's visit will move forward.

Riko made his way to his chair and dropped into it with a huff of exasperation. The king had been working on getting Infanta Gina to Versuvia for weeks now. She was the latest candidate his father had in mind to be the next Princess Suarez.

A potential bride for Riko.

The urge to stride to his father's wing and demand he rescind the invitation was so powerful, Riko found himself at his door to do just that before he bit out a curse and returned to his chair.

What exactly would his argument be? That he had complicated feelings for the children's new nanny?

No, there was no way around it. Infanta Gina would be arriving to attend the Versuvia National Spirit Festival scheduled in a few weeks' time. And Riko would do his princely duties and entertain her as expected.

Hands shaking with frustration, he typed out a response to his father. The only response he could send.

Be there in twenty.

It wasn't as if he had a choice. The vision of Elle staring up at him in the maze just moments ago invaded his mind. Her eyes hooded, desire flooding her features. Desire for him.

He hadn't known her for long, but her face was imbedded in his mind. The hazel-green hue of her eyes, the slight upward tilt of her nose, how her hair changed color depending on how and where the light hit it.

By contrast, despite having run into her several times over the years, he'd be hard pressed to recall what the infanta so much as looked like.

Riko made his way to his father's quarters.

The family resemblance was unmistakable. Elle took in the two small faces looking up at her, full of curiosity and wonder. The Suarez genes were strong with these two. Poor Isabel. It appeared her children had inherited very little of their mom's features and quite the cornucopia from their father and uncle.

There she went again. Her thoughts seemed to drift to Riko all too often and much too easily. Being alone with him in the maze, feeling his closeness as they were completely isolated together. Anything could have happened. Heaven help her, she might have let it if she hadn't come to her senses in the nick of time.

Enough. Her sole focus had to be on the present moment. And meeting the children she'd be caring for, for the first time.

The little boy, Ramon, stepped forward with his hand extended toward her. "Pleased to meet you, ma'am. I'm Ramon. I'm six." After letting go of Elle's hand, he pointed to his sister. "This is Tatyana. She's four."

Elle resisted the urge to chuckle at the exaggerated politeness that bordered on formality coming from such a small human.

"Lovely to meet you both," she said, smiling wide.

The little girl stepped forward, her large brown eyes focused firmly on Elle's face. "I'm four," she declared loudly, holding up three fingers. "How many are you?"

Elle tapped her nose playfully. "Let's just say that to answer I would need all of my fingers and toes and a few more."

That earned her a childish giggle. Elle crouched to get closer to the children's level. "Now that I know how old you both are and your names, why don't you tell me something else about yourselves."

Ramon stepped closer, an excited smile lighting up his face. "I like to play baseball. Like they do in 'Merica."

"That's lovely. Maybe we can play sometimes. I used to play with my sisters in the summer. Back in 'Merica."

Ramon clasped his hands together, excitement flooding his features. Any sense of formality had been completely replaced by pure childish thrill. "Oh, please. Oh, please. Oh, please."

This time Elle didn't bother hiding her chuckle. "You got it. First chance we get outside."

Ramon mimicked swinging a bat then celebrating a successful hit. Elle applauded the pretend home run before turning her attention to Tatyana. "What about you? Is there anything you like to do?"

The little girl nodded enthusiastically, her small chin hitting her chest. "I like stories. Mama reads to me. So does Papa."

"How fun. We can certainly do that too.

Maybe we can even make up some stories of our own. Would that be fun?"

"Sí!" Both children answered at once.

Elle sat all the way down on her bottom. "Would you like to do that now? Come up with our own story? We could even act it out. Like a play."

She appeared to have their full attention now. Tatyana was practically squealing with excitement, and Ramon stood grinning from ear to ear.

Well, that would take care of the afternoon's activities. "Ramon, would you get me that large pad off the easel in the corner? And a big marker?"

The little boy ran to do as he was told while Tatyana surprised her by climbing onto her lap. Within minutes, the three of them had entered a made-up world full of fairies and rainbows and one very mischievous unicorn.

Not a bad way to start her first day with the children. And not a bad way to keep thoughts of Riko below the surface. For now.

An hour after leaving his parents' wing, Riko wondered if it was too early to pour a stiff drink of *herbero*. The conversation with his father had gone about as well as he'd expected.

Despite Riko's attempts to push back, the

king was determined that the formal visit of Infanta Gina move forward as planned. No amount of argument would change his mind.

Riko was usually careful about picking his battles with the king. But this morning he'd fought particularly hard. To no avail.

He needed a distraction. A punishing run along the beach was always an option to vent some frustration. Maybe he'd invite his brother along for a little friendly competition. Manny had beat him the last time; it was time Riko rectified the loss with a challenge to a rematch.

He went in search of his brother only to be the distracted by a squeal of delight coming from the playroom once he reached the Granada wing. That was definitely his niece. And apparently she was having the time of her life, whatever she was doing.

He would have never guessed. The scene that greeted him when he reached the playroom's doorway had Riko doing a double take.

Elle stood in the center of the room dressed as some kind of pirate with his niece and nephew in similar costumes. They were acting out some sort of skit to an audience of Riko's family members. He had to blink to make sure he wasn't seeing things. Was that really his mother and father clapping and laughing to the antics of the three performers before them? His father complained bitterly about having to attend any kind of theater. Yet here he was, paying rapt attention, a wide smile on his face.

Even Isabel was there, upright in a rocking chair, a crocheted blanket covering her lap. Manny stood behind her, his hands on her shoulders while he watched his children and their new nanny act out what was clearly a scene written by the children.

No one even noticed Riko standing off to the side, so engrossed in the little "play" as they were. Finally, Manny looked in his direction but before he could wave him over, Riko gave a small shake of his head to not give him away. He didn't want to disrupt the delightful moment.

His brother turned his attention back to the entertainment, giving his wife's shoulders a little squeeze.

After delivering a few more lines, Elle took the children's hands in her own and they sang a short song Riko guessed was the finale. Afterward, the three of them took a bow. The other adults responded with raucous applause and a standing ovation. Riko joined in, first clapping then with a crescendo of a whistle.

Elle's smile froze on her face and her head

whipped in his direction. As he'd intended, she'd had no idea he'd been there.

The shocked expression on her face left no doubt about it.

CHAPTER FOUR

ELLE STOOD FROZEN in her spot, her smile unmoving. How long had Riko been standing there? How had she not noticed his presence? Up until now she'd always been so aware of him. She'd been preoccupied with their little play, anxious beyond words that the king and queen had appeared out of nowhere to watch the little skit Elle had the children create as a way of getting to know them.

Just when she'd gotten her heart rate down enough to actually get through and complete the silly little performance, it had skyrocketed again. Thanks to Riko.

"Bravo!" Prince Manuel shouted, approaching her and clapping. Then he ducked and embraced both of his children in turn. "Who knew you two were such talented thespians."

The queen smiled at her grandchildren. "Indeed, that was quite entertaining, my darlings." She tucked her hand in her husband's elbow.

"Thank you all for such a fun display." With that, the two of them walked out of the room.

Little Tatyana ran over to where her mother sat. "Did you like it, Mama?"

Isabel tousled her daughter's hair affectionately. "I absolutely adored it."

Manny returned to his wife's chair and reached for her hand. "I'm glad to hear it, *mi amore*. But I think it's time we get you back to bed. That's enough excitement for one day."

Isabel waved his words away. "I'm fine, Manny. You don't need to be quite so babying," she admonished but with zero venom in her voice.

Manny didn't argue any longer, simply leaned over and lifted his wife gingerly in his arms then began to carry her out of the room.

"Come, you two," he addressed his children over his shoulder. "Help me tuck your mother back into bed." The children followed them, giggling and poking each other playfully.

Which left only her and Riko. Elle swallowed. She hadn't forgotten what had happened the last time they were alone together. In fact, she couldn't get it out of her mind.

"Well done, Señorita Stanton. Color me impressed."

"Thanks. The children came up with the story. They're really quite delightful."

He smiled at her. "I was more so referring to how you seem to have won over my mother and father within hours of arriving. No small accomplishment."

If he only knew. Elle's nerves had gone tighter than a stretched rubber band when the senior royal couple had arrived. "I was petrified. I've never performed in front of an actual king and queen before. Not that it was any kind of real acting I was doing."

"Well, you've clearly won them over."

Elle tried to take the compliment to heart. But she was still nervous about what Riko's family might think of her. So far, so good, it appeared. But she couldn't get too comfortable. She needed this job. And the complication that was her growing attraction to the man standing before her was just that. A complication. One that she couldn't let distract her.

A good start would be to extricate herself from this room and away from his presence.

"If you'll excuse me," she began. "I'll go see about the children."

Riko stopped her with a hand gently on her forearm before she could take a step. "You have some time. The children tend to crawl into bed with their mother around this time of day and they all nap."

"Oh, I didn't realize." There went her excuse

to step away from Riko and the temptation that hummed through her entire body whenever he was in close proximity. "I guess I'll just head to my room then until they're ready for me."

He crossed his arms over his chest. "You could do that. But it occurred to me that when I pulled you away from Maribel earlier today, it probably disrupted the schedule set up for you. For instance, have you eaten?"

She had not. In all the excitement since she'd arrived at the castle, it hadn't occurred to her to see about doing so. But now that Riko mentioned it, Elle realized she was downright famished. As if in response, her stomach let out a low growl, clearly audible in the silence of the room. Elle wanted to sink to the floor in embarrassment. This man was probably used to being around the most graceful, most polished women in the world. And here she was, with her stomach loudly grumbling in his presence.

"I guess I'm hungrier than I might have guessed."

Riko threw his head back and released an amused chuckle. "Here." He extended his hand to her. "Follow me. I'll show you to the kitchens and introduce you to the culinary staff."

Elle scrambled for an excuse to turn down his offer. Hadn't she sworn down in the garden that she would do her best to stay away from him? Though she really was rather famished. It wouldn't do for her to faint from hunger on her first day on duty, would it?

Besides, Riko was just being polite. He probably felt responsible for her until she became more comfortable in her new role and with her new surroundings.

They took the same elevator down to the main floor then Riko led her down yet another hallway. She was going to need a detailed map of this place if she had any hope of not getting lost. Honestly, the Suarez castle had to be bigger than the world-class resort on Majorca she'd been just been fired from.

Was that really less than a week ago? It seemed like another lifetime, another reality. Majorca was only a short boat ride away, but once again Elle felt as if she was in a completely different world.

He couldn't very well have had her go hungry. Especially considering he was the reason she'd missed lunch.

As he led Elle through the main dining hall and past the wide stainless-steel doors of the primary kitchen, Riko knew he was only trying to justify commandeering Elle when he'd so recently sworn to himself that he would try to keep his distance.

His phone vibrated in his pocket for an incoming call.

It was Maribel. "Sorry to disturb you, sir. I wondered if you knew where the new nanny might be. I wanted to see if she might be ready for lunch and then a tour of the rest of the palace."

The right thing to do would be to just tell Maribel to come to the kitchen and take over Elle's lunch and touring. But he couldn't seem to bring himself to say the words. Besides, he was already here. What would be the sense in making the other woman go out of her way when he was perfectly capable of the task at hand? Nothing said he and Elle couldn't be on friendly terms. Riko was simply showing his friend where to find something to eat.

"I'm handling it, Maribel. You may tend to your other duties."

A long pause on the other end of the line told him he'd surprised the woman once more. It took a while longer before she answered him. "Oh, I see. In that case, Your Highness, there is a tray prepared for her in the secondary pantry. I'm sure one of the sous-chefs will be able to retrieve it for her."

"I'm sure we'll be able to locate it. Thank you."

"If it's all right," Elle was saying, "I thought

I might head outdoors to get some fresh air while I eat."

"That sounds like a lovely idea," he answered. "I can point you to the perfect spot. The patio by the south garden would be perfect on a sunny day such as this one. It even offers a majestic view of the ocean in the distance."

Her eyes lit up. "Would you? Or perhaps you could…"

"What is it?" he asked when she hesitated.

Elle gave a brisk shake of her head. "Nothing. Never mind. It would be too presumptuous of me to ask," she added almost under her breath.

Riko had no doubt what she wasn't risking to ask. She didn't want to eat alone.

What was the harm in joining her? Would it be so bad for him to actually get outdoors during the day, take his midday meal outside until his next international call later this afternoon? Something so simple; eating his lunch outside. Riko couldn't remember the last time he'd done so. Not since he was a child.

And it wasn't as if Elle had any friends in Versuvia just yet. So the two of them enjoying a friendly lunch together was nothing to get worked up about. Besides, what kind of gentleman would he be if he turned down her

Invitation for a simple picnic lunch her first day here?

"Listen, as it so happens—" he patted his middle for added effect "—I haven't had lunch yet either."

She tilted her head, studying him with a small knowing smile. "Is that so?"

"Would you mind some company while you eat?"

The smile widened. "I would like that very much, Riko."

The way she said his name sent an unfamiliar sensation down his spine.

"No. Thank *you*. I wasn't really looking forward to sitting alone at my desk with a sandwich. This will be an unexpected treat."

Her expression told him she wasn't buying it for a minute. But she didn't say anything, simply followed him to the pantry. Just as Maribel had told him, there was a tray set up with a variety of breads and small tapas dishes, each individually wrapped. A placard with Elle's name etched on it sat on the rack in front.

"Looks like the staff prepared this for you," he told her.

"Wow. That's quite the feast."

"Does that mean you won't mind sharing?"

She laughed. "It would only go to waste if I

didn't. We'll probably still have some left over even with the two of us eating."

"Speak for yourself. I happen to be famished. You have no idea the extent of my appetites."

He could have sworn he heard her suck in a breath. Now why had he said it like that? His wording could definitely be interpreted as some kind of double entendre. Granted, it was the direction his thoughts had been heading all day. But he certainly hadn't meant to voice them out loud. Apparently, his subconscious had other ideas.

Riko pushed past the sudden awkwardness in the air by taking hold of the serving tray and pulling it out of the pantry.

He glanced around for a moment, not finding what he was looking for. "What?" Elle asked.

"Maribel usually serves some type of sparkling water with lunch. I'm wondering where that might be."

She tilted her head. "Sparkling water is usually served cold. So my guess would be that it's in the fridge."

Perfectly reasonable assumption. He just needed to ascertain where the fridge might be.

"You do know where the refrigerator is, don't you?"

He wiggled his eyebrows at her in answer.

He had no clue. "Aren't those large rectangular appliances that store food?" he asked in an exaggerated tone.

She laughed at that. He could really get used to that laugh of hers. Something dipped in the pit of his stomach whenever he heard it.

"Have you ever even been in here before?" she asked with a playful smile.

"Of course I have. Several times. And each time I was promptly told to leave and that I was in everyone's way as they were trying to prepare the meal. Though in a much more disguised and polite way."

She stepped out of the pantry and crossed the room to another set of doors. "May I?" she asked, reaching for the handle.

"Be my guest."

She pulled one of the doors open and a slight mist of frost drifted above her head.

Huh. Had the palace always had a walk-in refrigerator?

Elle disappeared inside then came back out with two glass bottles. "Bingo," she said, holding up her bounty.

Within moments they were seated at the wicker table on the patio, the bright rays of the sun blocked by a sizable canvas umbrella. Elle unwrapped both sandwiches as he twisted off the caps on the bottles.

"It's absolutely lovely out here," she remarked in between bites.

"Wait until you see it all decked out and decorated for the National Spirit Festival."

"The spirit festival?"

He nodded, swallowed the morsel in his mouth. "It's a yearly tradition the beginning of every summer. Versuvians as well as guests from all over the world will be in attendance."

One of those distinguished guests happened to be a candidate for his hand in marriage. But Elle didn't need to know about that right this moment.

He would tell her. Of course, he would. Only not right now. They were just friends, after all. And he was enjoying her company too much to broach the subject.

First thing tomorrow morning, before Elle started her day, he would stop by and mention that a prominent Spanish noble would be attending the festivities on the personal invitation of the royal family in the hopes that Riko and she would hit it off and the wheels of matrimony would be set in motion. He would also make sure to explain to her that, if given any kind of choice on his part, no such visit would be taking place. That it was singularly the will of the king and queen.

Elle deserved to hear all that from his lips

and no one else's. As his friend. He would tell her, he vowed, first thing in the morning.

Elle lay on the most comfortable bed she'd ever had the luxury to sleep on. Although she hadn't done much sleeping despite the fluffy soft mattress beneath her. She tossed from side to side for what had to be at least the dozenth time and groaned in frustration. She wasn't typically prone to insomnia but tonight she couldn't seem to drift off, despite the incredibly long and eventful day she'd just lived through.

The problem was one handsome prince she couldn't seem to get out of her mind. Whenever she closed her eyes, his dark features floated in her mind. The moments she'd spent with him since arriving, every second of their time together lingered in her consciousness. The feel of his palm against the small of her back as he led her around the castle, the slight curve of his lips when he smiled at her, the scent of him.

She couldn't have imagined the desire in his eyes while in the maze, when he'd leaned closer, his breath hot against her cheek. For one ridiculous moment, she thought about letting him kiss her. Maybe she should have. As foolish as it would be to open her heart to someone so inaccessible, it might have been worth the risk of consequences just to be able to taste the man. If only just the once.

Tossing onto her back, she blew out a long, exasperated sigh. She was being fanciful and silly. What was the point of such childish imaginings? She was here to do a job that Riko had been kind enough to arrange for her. Of course she was attracted to him. But she couldn't jeopardize her position as the family's nanny by entertaining lusty thoughts about the future king. Especially while knowing full well that any kind of future with said heir to the throne was an impossibility.

Right now, she desperately needed to get some sleep or she would be useless the following day. Not a good way to start in her new role. The children were absolute darlings from what she'd seen of them so far. But they were spirited and full of energy. Elle would need to be primed and ready if she wanted any hope of keeping up with them.

Plus she was to meet with Isabel first thing in the morning to go over all her responsibilities. Appearing before the princess droopy eyed and tired wouldn't do at all. Was it against protocol to yawn in front of royalty?

A glance at the bedside clock told her it was almost two in the morning. Elle groaned out loud and rubbed her eyes, willing for sleep to come. But it was no use. She'd barely dozed off when her phone alarm rang six hours later.

Elle groaned and turned to her side. How was it morning and time to face the day already?

First things first; she would need coffee. A lot of it. After a quick shower in the private bathroom of her suite, she made her way downstairs and toward the kitchen. The last time she'd walked through these steel doors, Riko had been behind her, touching her, laughing with her.

Elle gave her head a brisk shake and pushed through the doors. She had to get that man out of her head or she was going to be utterly useless. Enough was enough.

"May I help you, miss?" An accented voice stopped her before she'd taken so much as a step into the room.

Elle turned to face a tall, mustached young man in a crisp white jacket and pressed black slacks.

"I was just looking for some coffee." She extended her hand. "I'm Elle, the children's new nanny. I'm afraid I'm still learning my way around."

He actually tapped his heels together! Just like in the movies. "Pleasure to meet you. I'm

Sebastian, one of the kitchen staff. Call me Seb. If you'll head back to your room, we'll have a tray delivered to you ASAP."

Oh, dear. Maybe she wasn't meant to be down here. Had she just broken some unspoken rule about being in the kitchens when she didn't work there? She was debating whether to apologize when Sebastian continued. "I will bring it up to you personally," he added with a charming smile. If Elle didn't know better, she may have thought he sounded somewhat flirtatious.

Just went to show, there were plenty of men in the proverbial sea. She really didn't need to spend her days and nights pining over one so far out of her reach.

"Thank you," she answered. "I look forward to it."

"As do I." He gave her a small bow.

When a knock sounded at her door about fifteen minutes later, Elle anxiously swung it open. Only, it wasn't the handsome, friendly staffer she'd met earlier. Riko stood smiling in the hallway. Despite herself, Elle's breath caught in her throat. He was dressed much more casually today. In a Henley type shirt with three buttons at the collar, a shade of green that brought out the dark tone of his hair and eyes. Even first thing in the morning, he looked so devilishly handsome she was having trouble concentrating.

"Good morning."

Between her surprise at seeing him at her door and the way he took her breath away, Elle was having trouble finding her voice.

His smile faded at her continued silence. "Everything all right?" he asked.

Elle managed to pull herself together. "Yes. Everything's fine. I was just expecting someone else."

He lifted an eyebrow. "Oh?"

As if on cue, Seb rounded the corner down the hall, pushing a tray cart full of dishes and one steaming silver carafe. He did a double take as he approached.

The man was just as surprised as she'd been to find the crown prince at her door.

CHAPTER FIVE

THIS WAS WHAT he got for being honorable. The urge to see Elle as soon as he had awoken had been impossible to ignore, despite the unpleasant task he had to see her for. Judging by the way this staff member with the rolling tray was staring at him with his mouth agape, he had to wonder if this was a good idea, after all. He should have found a less private spot to have the conversation about Gina's impending visit. He should have just asked her to meet him for coffee on the veranda.

Now, it appeared someone had already arranged for her to be served with a breakfast tray. Which left Riko standing in this hallway awkwardly while a kitchen staffer no doubt wondered why his prince was outside the door of another employee.

He swore silently under his breath. What if this man was reaching the disastrous conclusion that Riko might be leaving rather than just arriving at Elle's door? Great. He could just imagine the gossip fiasco that idea might generate within the palace walls.

The other man immediately stepped out from behind his trolley and gave Riko a bow. "Your Highness. I'm so terribly sorry. I didn't realize I'd be delivering a serving for two. I'll go remedy that right away."

Riko stopped him before he could turn back around and leave. "That won't be necessary. I don't intend to stay." He turned back to face Elle. "I was just stopping by on my way to my office to see how the palace's latest hire had fared on her first day and night. I won't be here long."

Elle's lips tightened into a thin line before she spoke. "How very kind of you, Your Highness," she said, her voice stiff. "I had a very enjoyable first day and slept soundly." She'd never addressed him quite so formally before. But he didn't have the luxury of exploring why right now.

"Glad to hear it, Ms. Stanton," he answered. Probably best to refer to her by her surname, given that they had an audience. He shot her what he hoped was an apologetic look before turning to leave. The staffer gave him one more bow as Riko walked past.

Well, that hadn't turned out at all the way

he'd imagined. He hadn't even managed to tell her about Infanta Gina. Riko heard the staffer's voice shortly after he rounded the corner.

"Wow. That was unexpected," the man said. "It isn't often the prince himself checks on a new hire personally."

If he wasn't mistaken, there was a level of familiarity in his tone. When exactly had Elle met this man?

Riko couldn't help but linger. Though the impropriety of the situation wasn't lost on him. He was actually eavesdropping. How unbecoming of someone in his position.

Elle's voice sounded tight when she answered. "Probably because he happened to hire me himself. I'm sure that's the only reason."

Did she really believe that? She sounded so convincing. So convinced.

"You didn't need to bring all this up for me personally," he heard her tell the other man.

"But I promised to do just that. What kind of man would I be if I went back on my word?"

Elle's soft laughter echoed down the hall, and Riko felt his jaw tighten. This man was clearly flirting with her. And she sounded as if she was enjoying it.

"I also had an ulterior motive."

Riko's pulse picked up. He knew he should move on and stop listening, but there was no way he was going to miss the rest. Ulterior motive, indeed.

"You did?" Elle asked.

"That's right. The kitchen staff and a few others typically get together late in the evening for a bite and a quick drink at the beach after our shifts. I wanted to see if you'd like to join us tonight."

Riko silently willed her to turn him down, to say no. Despite how selfish it was of him to wish such a thing. But Elle's response was almost immediate.

"I'd like that very much. Thank you."

"My pleasure."

It certainly was. This server sounded beyond pleased. Riko could just imagine the satisfaction on the man's face as he stared at Elle. He was no doubt admiring the thick curls of her fiery red hair that she wore in a loose bun atop her head this morning. The way the color of her tank top brought out the highlights in those curls and showed off her slight tan. Riko had half a mind to turn right back around and interrupt them, stop their conversation before it could go any further.

Stop.

It was no concern of his. Elle was the type to make friends and attract suitors. As pretty and outgoing as she was, what human male

with breath in his lungs wouldn't take the opportunity to invite her to events and try to get
to know her better. Wasn't that exactly what
he'd been doing?

And he had absolutely no standing to do so.
Certainly less so than the man she was currently speaking with. He was due to entertain
the infanta in just a couple of weeks. A woman
who might very well become the wife his parents wanted by his side.

He had no right to resent what he was hearing between Elle and this staffer. And he certainly had no right to stand here and continue
listening.

With great reluctance, he forced his feet
to move down the hall to his study to finally
begin some work.

It was going to be a long day. His focus was
sure to be shot for the rest of the morning. If
not the entire day and into the night, when Elle
would be joining her new friends on the beach.

He'd behaved like a completely different person. Elle wanted to believe she might have
imagined it, but there was no use denying it.
Riko had been very careful to keep his distance this morning when he'd come to see her.
Both literally and figuratively. The way he'd
answered Seb when the other man had asked

about bringing up another breakfast for him left no room for error regarding exactly who she was to him. And here she'd thought maybe they were becoming friends.

Ha! Served her right for even going there. He was heir to a throne. While she was simply a palace employee.

Elle scurried out of the elevator and down the hallway to the room she'd been told was Isabel's. She wasn't running late, but she didn't want to risk running into some kind of delay along the way. This was her first one-on-one meeting with the children's mother, and she wanted things to go smoothly. It was going to be hard enough to stay focused, between her sleepless night and the way the events of the morning kept replaying in her head.

Didn't her father always say her lack of focus was her biggest flaw? Or was it her lack of drive he kept harping on? Probably both.

When she reached and knocked on Isabel's door, she got an immediate response to enter. The princess was propped up on a large four-poster bed when Elle stepped into the room and shut the door behind her.

Isabel's ebony hair fell in waves over her shoulders; a thin crochet blanket covered her up to her waist. Even on bed rest, the woman was stunning. Despite the dark circles under her eyes, and the tight lines around her mouth, Isabel struck a commanding picture. Now this was the type of woman a royal prince fell for and wed.

Isabel offered her a friendly smile and waved her closer. "Come, Elle. Sit and let's chat for a bit," she said in a soft friendly voice.

Elle pulled over the only chair in the room that looked movable.

"I must apologize for being so ill prepared for your arrival," Isabel said, adjusting the pillow behind her to sit straighter.

Elle was taken aback by her words. She hadn't been expecting an apology from a member of the royal family.

Isabel continued. "My pregnancy has not been a smooth one, and I'm a bit less organized than usual."

"Your Highness, there is no need to apologize."

"You must call me Isabel, please."

"If you insist."

The princess nodded once. "I do. And if you won't hear of an apology then at least allow me to thank you for coming to our aid on such short notice. We are so fortunate Riko found you when he did."

"I'm the one who's fortunate, Your Hi—" Elle caught herself. "Isabel," she corrected.

"Riko was beyond generous to arrange for my employment."

"Well, you did save him from drowning. I'd say you're still in the lead." She chuckled softly. "To think, given the way he described the incident, we thought he'd imaged you. His recollection sounded preposterous with visions of a mermaid pulling him out of the water."

"I imagine some confusion is fairly common after a traumatic incident," Elle said, though it did strike her ego ever so slightly that Riko had such a hazy recollection of her from that moment.

"Well, however much he remembers, he's spoken so highly of you. I've never heard him sing anyone's praises quite so effusively."

Elle couldn't help but feel touched at those words. Still, be that as it may, Isabel was referring to the same man who'd earlier acted as if he barely knew her.

"He's very kind to do so."

Isabel tilted her head, her eyes roaming over her. "Right. He is indeed a very kind man. Though I dare say, the regard he has for you seems to be particularly high. It's rather uncharacteristic of him to grow so fond of someone quite so quickly."

Elle shifted in her chair, unsure how to respond. As much as she wanted to take Isabel's words to heart, it would be dangerous to assume anything as far as Riko was concerned.

Luckily, Isabel changed the subject and shifted to the reason Elle was here. "Let's start with the children's schedule, shall we?"

Elle pulled her phone out of her pocket and clicked on the appropriate app then began taking notes. For the next several minutes, Isabel gave her detailed information about the children she'd be caring for over the next several weeks. It was clear that the woman was a very hands-on parent who loved her children dearly. It was hard not to compare that type of upbringing with the one she'd lived herself as a child. She and her sisters had had a revolving door of sitters and nannies with both parents much too busy to make time for family. Even vacations had been taken with paid strangers.

"To conclude," Isabel said, "I will warn you that my son and daughter are perilously close to being spoiled rotten, the way they're doted on by their father, grandparents and uncle. The latter being the worst offender."

That didn't surprise her in the least. Riko's eyes lit up with true affection whenever he spoke of his niece and nephew.

"So, you and I must be united in our efforts to curb all that spoiling, deal?"

Elle smiled and nodded. "Deal."

"And of course, you'll be accompanying them and helping to prep them for their roles in the National Spirit festivities. Has anyone mentioned that event to you at all?"

"Very briefly. And only in passing."

Isabel inhaled deeply then released a long breath. It was obvious she was beginning to tucker out. Elle didn't want the princess to overexert herself on Elle's account.

"But I know there's a detailed file about it in the laptop I was given. I'll be sure to study it while the children are taking their lessons this afternoon."

"Lovely. And perhaps Riko can fill you in on any missing pieces. The biggest concern with the children will be introducing them to all the special guests who will be in attendance. Not least the infanta."

A chill of trepidation ran down Elle's spine. She was about to hear something that would crush her, she just knew it. "Why her in particular?"

"In the event the king and queen get their wish and she's fast-tracked to become the children's auntie."

Auntie? But that would mean…

"She is a top candidate in their eyes as a potential future daughter-in-law," Isabel added, confirming Elle had been right to feel the apprehension spiking through her.

A brick dropped to the pit of her stomach and her vision blurred at Isabel's words. So part of this festival would involve matchmaking for the royal heir.

And Riko hadn't seen fit to mention it to her.

Elle tried in vain to stay involved in the conversation and listen intently to what Sebastian was telling her. But it was no use. Her mind was a mishmash of thoughts. Thoughts that centered around one main theme—Prince Eriko Rafael Suarez.

It had been a mistake to come to the staff beach party tonight. She didn't have the energy or the mental capacity to be sociable right now. Which was a shame. Everyone she'd met so far had been personable and friendly. Bouncy Spanish pop played from a speaker on the sand, with a small bonfire providing just the right amount of heat and light for the group of ten people gathered around it.

All the makings of a fun evening and she couldn't seem to enjoy it.

It didn't help that a lot of the conversation among the partygoers centered around the buzz about the potential new princess-slash-bride who'd be visiting within the week. Apparently, she was a highly accomplished musician with a litany of achievements and awards. With the beauty to match. She sounded perfect.

"So what do you think, Elle?" Sebastian ask.

Think about what? She hadn't even heard the last several things he'd said. "I think you're absolutely correct," she replied, hedging a chance that a universal answer might suffice to whatever his question had been about.

His expression told her she'd guessed wrong. He blinked at her in clear confusion. Then he tipped his head back and laughed out loud. "You seem a bit distracted. Does it have anything to do with your morning visitor?"

How obvious was she? While she scrambled for a response to that impossible question, Sebastian spared her the effort with his next words. "Let me just tell you, it's unheard-of for the prince to be checking in on a member of the staff. I've been working here for over five years and I've never heard of such a thing. He looked like the cat that had been caught with the canary when I turned that corner this morning."

Elle didn't have the wherewithal for the direction this conversation was headed in. Little did Seb know. "He's just being kind, Seb. He hired me personally and wants to make sure it works out." And no doubt, he felt responsible for her, given the way they'd met.

"Si usted lo dice…" he answered. She could guess what that meant. Right now, she just wanted to leave.

"It was so nice of you to invite me out, Seb. But my battery seems to be draining of all energy. If you'd please excuse me, I think I'm ready to call it a day and head back for some rest," she told him, then turned to wave at the others. Several voices responded with protests but she simply smiled and made a gesture of sleeping, closing her eyes with her hands cupped under her tilted head.

"Sure. I'll walk you back to the palace."

Elle lifted a hand to stop him. She didn't want to cut his night short on account of her sour mood. "No. That's not necessary. I know my way, and I'd hate to take you away from the gathering."

Seb gave a shrug of acceptance and leaned over to give her a friendly peck on the cheek. *"Buenas noches."*

Elle started making her way back, the castle lit up like Lake Shore Drive during Christmastime before her. What part of the building was Riko in right this moment? What might he be doing? Had he given her another thought all day?

What did any of those questions matter to her. They shouldn't. She shouldn't be wondering about him at all.

He hadn't mentioned that the woman his parents wanted him to consider marrying would be arriving in a few short days. Which Elle had no right to even be upset about. Riko didn't owe her that kind of personal information. She was essentially a palace employee, no different from the crowd she'd just been introduced to. The only reason Riko even knew her name was because he'd hired her himself after a chance encounter. An encounter he barely even remembered.

So that was quite enough of her constant girlish romanticizing of Riko.

Elle quickened her pace and summoned up all her resolve as she made her way up the long, paved roadway leading to the main doors. From now on, she was going to know her place. She'd make sure to go to the next staff beach party and she'd be much more outgoing than she'd been tonight. She worked for the royal family, and her rightful place was with the staff.

And she was absolutely going to stop obsessively thinking about Prince Eriko Suarez and imagining there was anything more between them than a simple contractual, professional relationship.

By the time she reached the doors and pulled them open, she was determined to keep to her new resolution no matter what it might take.

Her resolve was tested immediately. When she made it to the castle doors, she literally ran into the man.

CHAPTER SIX

RIKO GLANCED AT his watch yet again. Then he looked up at the tall mahogany grandfather clock that loomed by the doorway as if it might tell him something different.

Isabel had mentioned in passing that Elle had left the castle. His niece and nephew were already in bed at this hour. Which meant she'd taken the man's offer from this morning to join him at some kind of beach party the staff was attending. The same party where she'd be meeting up with the handsome staff member who'd personally delivered her breakfast this morning.

Well, good for her. Riko was glad she was getting acclimated and getting to know the others who worked at the palace. This was her personal time to do with as she wished. To spend with whoever she wished. And anyway, it was none of his concern, really. So why was he down here pacing the foyer instead of studying the spreadsheets that urgently required his attention before tomorrow morning?

Because he hadn't been able to concentrate on any of the numbers for more than a few seconds at a time. He'd nearly launched his tablet across the room and against the wall in frustration after his umpteenth attempt. For someone who normally prided himself on focus, it was beyond galling. All because he couldn't stop thinking about what Elle might be doing at that party and who she might be doing it with.

Maybe he'd take a walk along the beach. Though it was completely against protocol for him to try and crash a staff event, that wasn't necessarily what he'd be doing. It was a beautiful night, after all. Even the prince couldn't be faulted for wanting to get some air.

Who was he kidding?

The staffers would be suspicious; he'd never randomly appeared at one of their events before. And Elle would see right through him.

Riko bit out a curse and paced some more.

Then he made a decision. While he'd sensibly established that he couldn't very well crash this get-together, getting some air would actually do him some good. That's all he would do; he wouldn't even go near the beach where Elle might be with her new friends. Besides, he couldn't very well just stand here pacing a track on the Italian marble tiled floor. He didn't even want to think about the possibility of Manny appearing and asking him what he was up to. The teasing would never cease if his brother even suspected the source of Riko's agitation right now.

His mind made up, he strode to the door and yanked it open, startled to find Elle on the other side. Though "finding" wasn't quite the correct term. Rather, he caught her just as she was about to topple through the doorway.

"Oh!"

Riko took a moment to process what was happening. He'd just been agitated and pacing about, wondering what Elle was up to. Now, she was literally falling into his arms. It was almost an exact replay of what had happened yesterday in the maze.

She straightened, her eyes wide with shock. His arms were still wrapped around her waist and shoulders; he knew she'd regained her balance but hesitated letting her go just yet. She felt so right where she was. With him holding her, her skin warm everywhere it touched his.

"Uh, hi there," he finally managed to say. "Nice of you to drop in."

Pretty terrible attempt at humor, but he wasn't

exactly operating with all his wits about him at the moment.

"Riko. I…uh…was about to open the door when it disappeared from my grasp. I guess I lost my balance as a result."

He almost thanked her for doing so then stopped himself. How inappropriate. As was the way he still held her, tight against him in front of an open doorway right in the foyer where anyone could walk by. With great reluctance, he finally released her.

"I apologize," he began after the two beats it took regain his senses. "I didn't mean to startle or unbalance you. I was just headed out to get some air. Is that what you were doing?" he couldn't help but ask, though he knew he had no right to.

"No. Well, sort of. I was out with some other staffers. They were having a little get-together on the beach."

He made a show of lifting his wrist to look at his watch. Totally unnecessarily. He knew exactly what time it was; he'd been staring at his blasted watch for the past half hour. "Kind of early still."

She shrugged. "I just didn't have the energy or stamina. I had a bout of insomnia last night. I'm afraid it's finally caught up to me."

So, she'd been fibbing this morning when

she'd told him how well she'd slept. How curious. "Sorry to hear that. Was the bed or room not to your liking? We can see about other accommodations if that is the case."

She shook her head. "No. It was all lovely. One of the most comfortable beds I've ever slept on, in fact. That wasn't the issue," she said, not looking him in the eye for some reason.

"Glad to hear it. You know, we happen to have a cure-all for insomnia in this part of the world."

"You do?"

He nodded. "It's called horchata. A very soothing, warm drink that brings immediate calm."

"What is it?"

"Around here we like to make it with almond milk. Along with some real vanilla and a touch of cinnamon."

She licked her bottom lip at the description and he had to turn away. "That sounds delicious."

"We could try some now. There's always a pot of it brewed and kept warm in the sitting hall. If you're not too tired that is."

"Not too tired to turn down such a tempting sounding treat. But I don't want to impose on you. Didn't you say you were heading out to get some fresh air?"

If she only knew. The only reason Riko had

even felt a need to get out had been because he hadn't been able to stop thinking about her. Now, here she was. He couldn't very well tell her that, of course.

"Hmm. I did. But now I find myself craving the horchata I just told you about. But I might have a way to do both."

About ten minutes after she'd stumbled through the front doors and into Riko's arms, Elle found herself sitting outside under the sparkling stars. The veranda Riko had taken her to was expansive, decorated with several potted plants taller than even her companion. She could hear the ocean in the distance, the sea breeze carrying the scent of the sea and sand with it.

She took another sip of the horchata from her porcelain mug. Riko was right. It was delicious and went down smooth, in a calming and relaxing way. The taste of almonds and subtle vanilla lingered on her tongue after swallowing. The dusting of cinnamon added just the right amount of spice. Between the delicious soothing drink he'd served her and the romantic setting, she was finding it harder and harder to remind herself she was annoyed with him.

She had to wonder if he had any idea that

the palace staff was already speculating about the infanta who might be his intended.

"You appear deep in thought," he said, pulling her out of the questions running through her head. Questions that were beginning to dampen the tranquility she'd been enjoying up until they surfaced. "What are you thinking about?" he added after a beat.

If only she could tell him the truth. Somehow let him know that she was drawn to him in a way that both surprised and horrified her. That she was more aware of him than any man she'd ever encountered. The way the corners of his mouth crinkled when he flashed her that devilish smile. How he made her stomach flutter whenever he walked into the room.

How much it bothered her that he'd be entertaining a woman next week whom he'd most likely propose to.

No. She had to keep all that to herself. It was her burden to bear, the way she felt about him, how swiftly and strongly her feelings had developed in such a short time.

She offered a small fib instead as her answer. "I was just thinking how I haven't called my sisters in a while. They're probably getting antsy about my lack of contact."

"Hmm. You should remedy that first thing,

then. I myself am quite aware how pesky siblings can be."

She chuckled at that, relieved the conversation had steered toward a subject that allowed her to keep her head straight. "You and your brother seem close."

"Are you close with your sisters?"

She shrugged; the answer to that question was complicated. "Mostly. I'm the youngest of four. And they're all rather protective to the point where they can be a bit smothering."

He took another sip of his drink, his eyes trained on her over the rim of his cup. "Tell me about them."

Elle shifted in her chair. When he found out how accomplished her sisters were, she was going to appear so much less successful in comparison. She was proud of all her sisters, she really was. Loved them all dearly. It was just that her accomplishments were so trivial compared to all that her three older siblings had done. A fact not lost on their parents.

"Well, Maysie and Trina are doctors, like my mom. And Lizzie's an attorney like my father."

Riko merely lifted an eyebrow, so she continued. "I was supposed to follow in Lizzie's and my dad's footsteps and complete the circle."

"But that wasn't the life you wanted," Riko suggested.

Elle put her cup down, leaned her elbows on the table. "I tried. I really did. I studied international politics in college then applied to law schools throughout the Midwest. And then when the time came, I just couldn't do it."

"Let me guess. Your father was disappointed."

She nodded, her mind calling up the memories of that awful afternoon when she'd announced her intention to cease her studies. The looks of disappointment on her parents' faces. The disdain in their voice. Prominent attorney that he was, her father was impossible to argue with. She'd stammered and stuttered, sounding exactly like the scatterbrained young nitwit her parents were convinced she was.

"They both were, Mom and Dad. My sisters weren't exactly thrilled either. Turns out one's family isn't terribly enthusiastic when you announce that you're quitting school to join a traveling band to sing for a living. They were certain I was throwing my future away."

"But you did it anyway. You followed your dreams."

She had. Though she hadn't managed to achieve any level of success. "Maybe. But I didn't get very far. The band broke up. And I was on another continent from home with no other prospects. A complete failure."

His forehead creased. "You can't really think that."

"What other way is there to think? I fell flat on my face. Just like everyone warned me I would."

"Or you've hit a small obstacle until another opportunity comes along. In the meantime, you're gainfully employed helping to care for two children whose mother is temporarily not able to."

"It's kind of you to say that, Riko. Thank you."

He shrugged. "I only say it because it happens to be true."

"Unfortunately, my parents and sisters will not see things in quite so favorable a light. My last conversation with my father back in Majorca involved a lot of 'I told you so's."

"I'm sorry to hear that, Elle. He might come around."

She shook her head, sadness washing over her. In her father's eyes, she was a failure and probably always would be. "I don't think so. But thank you for trying to make me feel better. I've just come to accept that I'll never be the daughter my mother or father hoped that their youngest child could be. Certainly not comparable to their other children."

He released a long sigh. "Family expectations can be quite the burden, can't they?"

She studied him as a heaviness fell behind his eyes. "You sound like you might be speaking from experience."

She would be guessing correctly.

"I can't imagine having your parents also be your king and queen. What is it like?"

Riko wasn't sure how the subject matter had turned to him. Surprisingly, his first impulse wasn't to shut the conversation down as he normally would whenever he was asked a personal question. Instead, he found himself wanting to open up to Elle. To tell her exactly how heavy it weighed on him that he would be the inheriting the throne. To tell her how he'd been experiencing anxiety attacks ever since it had truly sunk into his brain that he would be the one leading this island kingdom someday soon. Attacks strong enough to wake him up at night.

Maybe it was the novelty of simply sitting with a friendly face, someone willing to listen who had no real connection to the royal family he was part of. He'd never had the pleasure of a casual conversation with a friend sitting outside on a pleasantly warm evening with the clear night sky overhead. Or maybe it was just so Elle could see she wasn't alone in the pressure that her family unduly forced on her. That sitting right across from her was a kindred spirit who could relate to such pressure.

But he couldn't deny that was only a portion of it. The rest was more selfish on his part. This was the most relaxed he'd felt since childhood. And it had everything to do with being in Elle's company.

He toyed with his cup, now empty, before answering her question. "It can feel overwhelming, to be honest," he confided, surprising himself some more. "It's much harder to defy your father when he also happens to be ruler of your nation. And your mother because she's also the queen."

Her eyes softened with understanding and sympathy. Which encouraged him to add, "So I just made sure to not defy them."

Then he went on. "I studied what they and the kingdom expected me to study. After university, I served in the Versuvian military, and I learned everything there was to know about Versuvia and its history."

"What did you want to study?" she asked.

"When I was very young and didn't know

any better, I liked to sketch and draw. If given the choice, I might have pursued architecture."

"But you weren't given the choice."

He shook his head. "I studied economics and European history instead. Just as my father did. Much more acceptable fields for future kings."

"Do you still sketch? Even just for fun?"

Riko blew out a puff of air. He couldn't remember the last time he'd held a pencil and clear sheet of sketch paper. "No. I put it behind me. What would be the use? Even if I wanted to, I would hardly have the free time."

"I'm sorry to hear that, Riko. That you had to give up something that you enjoyed and were talented at."

He chuckled at that. "I have no indication that I had any kind of talent. Didn't pursue it long enough to find out."

The small smile she gave him made him want to reach over the table and take her hand in his. He leaned back in his chair instead, increasing the distance between them before he gave in to such an impulsive and foolish urge.

"I have no doubt you're talented. You seem to be good at a lot of things." She looked down after speaking, as if surprised she'd said the words.

Riko cleared his throat, disarmingly touched by the statement.

The conversation was a getting a bit too heavy, and he was getting dangerously close to sounding like a poor, self-pitying prince when he had a life more privileged than most, so Riko decided a change of subject was in order.

"If only Manny had had the courtesy to arrive first by mere minutes, he would have been the one to deal with all the protocol and expectations, leaving me to a life of carefree luxury."

She laughed. "I agree. That was very rude of him."

"Well, he's always been rather inconsiderate. Isabel is a saint for putting up with him. The children definitely take after her. Luckily." He offered a silent apology to his brother for using him as a distraction in such a ridiculing way. Manny would understand if he were here.

"Well, your brother has been lovely to me so far. As has Princess Isabel. And the children are absolute delights. They're quite looking forward to the national day festivities." The smile faded from her face and her voice caught as she mentioned the event. She ducked her head before continuing. "I understand there will be visitors arriving from all over Europe to join the celebrations."

When she looked back up again, the reason for her question hit Riko square in the chest. She'd heard about Infanta Gina and why she would be arriving in Versuvia in a few days. He should have found a way to tell her himself after being thwarted that morning at her door by the staffer. Foolish of him to not think that it would come up in her conversations with others. For all he knew, the staffer was the one who let the cat out of the bag, trying to get into Elle's good graces by showing off how well informed he was.

First things first. He had to make amends with Elle.

A torrent of conflicting emotions collided in his chest. That Elle might be affected at the thought of him spending time with someone else warred with the truth that he had no right to feel any kind of pleasure at that knowledge. Added was the guilt that she'd had to find out from someone else. He felt like a heel in more ways than one.

"Elle, every once in a while my father insists on having me entertain someone he refers to as 'fitting.' As modern and progressive as he is, there are certain things he's still rather traditional about." Stubbornly so, he added silently.

She held a hand up before he could continue.

"You don't have to explain anything to me, Riko."

Maybe she was right. The only problem was, he wanted so badly to do exactly that.

CHAPTER SEVEN

THE FIRST DAY of the National Spirit Festival always seemed to bring on a buzz of excitement throughout the kingdom. Riko felt it in the air as soon as he began his morning.

The text from his father that had been waiting for him when he'd awoken served to further heighten his spirits. Apparently, Infanta Gina would have to delay her arrival due to a labor dispute within her country's borders. She wasn't sure how long she might be put off as she mediated the negotiations.

Riko had nothing against the woman. In fact, the few brief interactions he'd had with her in the past had been perfectly pleasant. And he certainly hoped any strife within her nation was resolved quickly so that she may travel again. He just hadn't been terribly enthusiastic about her arrival. He'd wanted to be able to enjoy the day of festivities without having to play charming suitor under his dad's scrutiny. Was that wrong of him?

Not if he kept those thoughts to himself, he figured.

A nagging voice in the back of his mind teased that he had a deeper reason for wanting to be free of the infanta a little longer. One that brought to mind hazel-green eyes and wavy red hair.

He pushed that thought aside.

The celebrations would start late morning with games and activities set up on the palace grounds for young children. He and Manny along with his parents always gave out prizes to the winners of various games and challenges. A few of which he even participated in.

Of course, Elle would have to be there to accompany his niece and nephew. He hadn't seen her since their time on the veranda. He had to wonder if that was by her design. Did she regret the way they'd confided in each other?

Just as well. As much as he enjoyed her company, he had no right to seek it. Now that Elle was acclimated in her new role and her place at the palace, there was no reason to keep checking on her.

A sinking feeling manifested in the vicinity of his heart. He hadn't intended it, but he'd grown quite fond of Elle's company. Being with her felt freeing and easy. As if he could be his true self without fear of dropping the prince face mask. In a different reality, he would have pursued what it meant that Elle invoked such carefree feelings in him.

Still, he didn't regret a single minute of that time on the veranda with Elle, simply chatting. Today, he'd take the opportunity to speak to her again about what the deal was with Infanta Gina. That he had nothing to do with her impending visit. The king had made the arrangements with zero input from Riko. Maybe he was being presumptuous in assuming that Elle should know that. But be that as it may, it was important to Riko for her to know it.

When he made it out to the grounds, there was already a flurry of activity. Several stands had been set up. The obstacle course and path for the three-legged race were arranged in their usual spots in the middle of everything. A deejay was setting up across the square near a temporary wooden stage and in front of an impromptu dance floor. There'd be music and dancing all day.

Riko was looking forward to it all even more so than usual. A large part of that could be attributed to seeing Elle's reaction to it. What was she like when she was simply having fun? He wanted badly to find out.

As if he'd summoned her with his thoughts, Riko sensed the moment Elle stepped outside. He turned to greet her, beyond pleased with the look on her face.

"Oh, my," she said breathlessly when she reached his side. "I came out to see what all the commotion and noise was that I'd been hearing since the wee hours."

"Good morning."

"Morning. This is quite the production."

"Just wait until it's in full swing."

She smiled, scanning the grounds. "Well, there are two little ones inside having breakfast that are having a great deal of trouble waiting for it." Her smile faded. "It's too bad Isabel can't participate. She's been talking about it endlessly."

"I'm sure Manny will figure out a way for her to at least watch some of the events," he reassured her.

"I hope so. The children are beyond excited about the day, but Tatyana in particular seems sad that Isabel won't be able to take part."

"It's a good thing they have you to step in."

"Care to tell me exactly what I'm in for?"

Riko gestured toward the obstacle course. "Well, I have no doubt you'll be dragged into both those races. Will absolutely have to get your face painted." He pointed toward the stage. "Plus there's a lot of dancing in your future. And food. Lots and lots of food. There'll be everything from empanadas to flan."

Elle laughed. "I think I can handle all that. Though the children are going to be exhausted."

"As will you."

She chuckled once more, and the tightness that had grown in his chest at the thought that Elle had been avoiding him loosened.

She looked away, her gaze focused on the field before she spoke. "But won't you be too busy entertaining the infanta once she arrives?"

"Turns out Infanta Gina will not make it today, after all. She sent her deep regrets and is not quite certain when she might arrive."

If Elle had any kind of reaction to that bit of news, she managed to conceal it completely.

"I hope everything is all right," she said after several beats of silence. Riko had been about to ask if she'd even heard him.

"Nothing concerning. She's just busy with some official business that's keeping her from leaving the country just yet. I'll be free to roam around and enjoy the festivities with everyone else all day."

"I see."

Again, he waited for some kind of real reaction. Once again, he waited in vain.

* * *

She had to get her inconvenient jealousy in check. Elle strode through the main hallway and toward the children's dining area trying to get her breathing under control. The amount of relief and giddiness she'd just experienced upon learning that Infanta Gina wouldn't be arriving today had shocked her through to her core.

She'd had no idea how badly she'd been dreading the infanta's visit. The sight of Riko accompanying her around the palace, how he'd grant her all his attention…

Despite herself, she'd spent a considerable portion of her evening the previous night scrolling through social media posts about the woman. She looked more and more beautiful with each photo Elle had found of her.

She'd made sure to avoid Riko these past few days to get used to the idea that she'd be staying away from him once his guest arrived. Now, given the reprieve, Elle wasn't sure how to react. After all, the reprieve was only temporary. Infanta Gina would be here soon enough.

Then she'd have to go through the same dread that she'd been dealing with all over again. No, best to stick to her original plan to stay away from Riko. She could do it if she really set her mind to it.

Two hours later, Elle realized just how wrong she'd been to think that. Her plan was utterly doomed to fail. She didn't stand a chance.

The children made a beeline for their uncle the moment they saw him upon arriving at the festival, which was now in full swing. It appeared the entire kingdom was on the palace grounds. Hordes of children ran around, loud bouncy music echoed through the air and some kind of folk dance performance was happening on the stage with a line of dancers in full costume. She had no choice but to follow Ramon and Tatyana to where Riko stood in the center of it all. He was dressed much more casually than usual in a pair of tan slacks and a V-neck sky blue short-sleeved top that fit him like a glove and showed off his toned chest and muscular arms.

Stop it.

"Uncle Riko!" Riko's face broke into a wide smile as soon as he saw them. Bending down, he somehow managed to grab hold of both children and lift them in the air to loud shrieks of delight before lowering them to the ground.

Elle stifled a gasp at the image. The man would make a wonderful father someday. Oh, dear. That was exactly the type of thought she had to make sure to avoid. True or not.

"This is quite the gathering," she said when she reached them.

"Trust me, it's just getting started," Riko answered, while simultaneously tousling his nephew's hair.

"Uncle Riko, I bet I can beat you at the crown toss again this year," Ramon declared, tugging on his uncle's pant leg.

"I wouldn't be so sure about that, little man," Riko answered, with mock seriousness.

"Let's go see!" Ramon demanded, not waiting for an answer as he turned and ran to a gold canvas tent that had all sorts of games set up inside.

"I wanna try too," Tatyana shouted, following her brother.

Riko and Elle trailed behind. "Beat you again? You let him win, don't you?" Elle asked needlessly. She was pretty sure she knew the answer.

"Maybe," he answered in a hushed tone. "Or maybe I just have really bad aim."

"Sure you do." She highly doubted it. From what she'd seen so far, Eriko Suarez wasn't bad at anything.

Sure enough, when they reached the table with a slew of plastic crowns and a short pole in the center, Riko was comically off target. Ramon managed to toss the crown onto the pole after his tenth try.

"I won! I won!" the little boy shouted, pumping his fist and earning a laugh from his uncle. Tatyana had seemingly forgotten the object of the game and was simply putting the crowns on her head.

"Let's do the leg race now!" Ramon shouted, running out of the tent and across the field to where several people were already gathered.

Ramon picked up one of the burlap sacks lying on the ground and stuck one leg in. His sister ran over to join him and did the same, sticking her leg in the same sack her brother had stepped into.

Elle's stomach froze as she realized what was bound to happen next. If Ramon and Tatyana were sharing a sack, and Riko intended to race too, then that would mean...

"Come on, Elle," Riko said, bending to retrieve one of the empty bags and stepping his right foot into it. "We'll have to let them win this too." He motioned to her left leg.

Elle thought about saying no, desperately wanted to do just that. But then she looked at the expectant faces of the two children. Their smiles as they waited patiently for her to do as Riko asked.

It was just a silly race. She could do this. They wouldn't even really be running; he was going to allow the children to win. If she was lucky, they wouldn't take more than a step or two. That had to be what Riko was thinking. It made sense. With a deep breath, she stepped into the bag and tried in vain to ignore the warmth of Riko's body so close to hers. The scent of him filling her nostrils.

A horn sounded behind them and the children took off. To her shock, Riko did the same. He apparently had no intention of going slowly. Elle wasn't prepared. She tried her best to keep up, but it was no use. They'd only gone three or four steps when she completely lost her balance. She was going down, and she'd be taking Riko with her. There was no way to stop it.

The next instant, she felt a pair of strong arms wrap around her waist. Instead of the impact with the ground she'd been expecting, she was cradled. Somehow Riko managed to catch her before she fell and twisted around so he would hit the ground first.

She landed square on top of him.

It took Riko several moments before he could catch his breath. Not necessarily because he'd just had the wind knocked out of him. No, it was more because of the woman sprawled over him. The same woman he hadn't been able to stop thinking about since he'd met her, the one who'd crept into his dreams at night and into his thoughts during his waking hours. Plenty of those thoughts had come up with exactly the scenario he was in right now—him flat on his back with Elle draped atop him.

Well, maybe not the exact scenario. Actually, the pictures in his mind had been quite different. Also, they hadn't been surrounded by laughing children with a crowd of other onlookers watching in amusement.

Elle appeared stunned, her wide eyes boring into his. Heaven help him, then those hazel-green eyes fell to his lips, desire and invitation clouding her irises. He gasped for the air that hadn't quite made it into his lungs yet. If it wasn't for their audience, he wouldn't hesitate to take her up on that invitation. And make a few of his own.

He couldn't be sure how much time went by. One thing he was certain of—he had no desire to let her out of his arms just yet, despite their surroundings.

Her tongue darted out to her lips and heat surged through his body. The way he reacted to this woman was nothing short of jolting. They were in the middle of a literal festival of people, and all his focus was squarely on her. Only her.

"Guess we lost the race, *cariña*," he said when he finally got his voice to work. The last word came out of its own volition. Darling, sweetheart. He'd never called her that before. He'd never called anyone that before.

Her eyes remained fixed on his, her lips parted. What if he just went for it? the devil on his shoulder asked. What if he just gave in to what he so badly wanted and just took her lips with his own? Despite the crowd, despite the flak that would be sure to follow. He could find a way to deal with the repercussions later. He had no doubt the taste of her would be worth it, even if just for a moment.

Elle's eyebrows lifted close to her hairline, as if she might have read his thoughts. Maybe she didn't need to. Perhaps they were written clearly on his face for anyone to see.

Her breath brushed against his chin in puffs. She felt soft and warm everywhere her body touched his. She scrambled in a futile effort to get off him. Of course, it was no use. They were literally tied together at a limb. The squirming only served to heighten his awareness of how intimate their position was.

The sudden sound of an airplane flying above was immediately followed by a chorus of cheers erupting around them. The skywriter. The king employed one every year on the first day to write patriotic message high among the clouds. The feat was one of the most anticipated events of the festival. Everyone anxiously waited to learn what this year's inspiring words might be. As far as Riko was concerned, he was just grateful for the distraction it provided at the moment.

Elle made yet another futile effort to flee. He stilled her with a finger under her chin, lifting her face to his. "Elle."

A glance around told him everyone's attention was still focused on the show overhead. All except for the two of them. They were so close now, a hair's width separated their faces. He couldn't take any more. He leaned even closer and brushed his lips to hers, ever so softly. Just enough to finally get the taste of her he'd been craving for so long. Without lingering he pulled back. Anyone watching would not have even noticed the subtle and rapid touch of his lips to hers.

Elle's eyes squeezed shut. She was trembling in his arms now just as he was shaking inside. Heaven help him, now that he'd tasted her, he couldn't wait to do it again.

"Do you two need a hand?"

Riko looked to the side to see a pair of athletic shoes about a foot away from his nose. Then he looked up to find Manny standing over them. Despite his question, it didn't appear he was at all ready to give them any kind of hand. His arms were crossed at his chest. A smirk on his face.

No doubt his brother found this very funny.

Riko ignored him and addressed Elle. "We have got to stop meeting like this," he said in an attempt to lighten the intensity of what had just happened.

Elle didn't bother to acknowledge his poor attempt at a joke. "Maybe if you tried to sit up," she offered.

He tried to do as she said, which only made things worse. To anyone watching, it would appear as if Elle was sitting on his lap. Thank heavens for the distraction of the skywriting show. Of course, Manny had somehow still managed to witness the debacle. Just like the typical thorn in Riko's side that he was.

His brother wasn't even trying to hide his amusement now. His smirk had grown into a wide grin. Riko figured it could be worse. It could be his mother or father standing above them watching this spectacle. Somehow, he didn't think the king or queen would be as amused by the scene as his brother seemed to be.

Elle's face was growing redder by the second. He did his best to kick off the sack. It had gotten good and tangled during their fall and subsequent struggle. Manny still made no effort to help. Darned if Riko was going to ask him to. Finally, the damn thing slipped off. Elle immediately jumped to her feet.

Shame. She had felt really good cradled in his arms, despite the circumstances that had brought her there. Her face was now the exact crimson of the carnation flowers that grew all over the island kingdom. "Elle," he began, not even certain what he would possibly say.

She didn't give him a chance to figure it out. "I'll go find the children," she announced, and practically bounded away.

Riko stood and brushed the dirt off his pants. His brother hadn't so much as moved. But he was now actively chuckling.

Riko glared at him. "You appeared to be enjoying that way too much."

"As did you, big brother," Manny said through his growing laughter.

CHAPTER EIGHT

She had to have imagined it. It couldn't have really happened. Riko hadn't just kissed her, slight as it had been, while she'd been sprawled on top of him. Heat still burned in her cheeks. Her body still held the warmth of his in every place they'd touched. Her lips still tingled with the taste of him.

Stop it.

She had to stop thinking about it. She had to stop thinking about him. The kiss didn't mean anything. It was barely even a kiss. A mere touching of his lips to hers. Soft and subtle.

So why was her stomach quaking like an active fault line? It had been foolish to go back on her original plan of trying to avoid Riko. She should have done exactly that. Even if the children dragged her to where he was, now she would keep her distance.

That meant no more races where they were tied together, for heaven's sake. Curse the complication that had delayed Infanta Gina's visit. Unlike Elle, the infanta would never get caught in such an undignified position. She probably had too much class. Too much grace.

Just like with her sisters, Elle couldn't compare.

And now she'd be thinking about that kiss to distraction. The last thing she needed. But it was impossible to get Riko out of her head while she could still taste him on her lips.

The rest of the afternoon into early evening passed by with her mind a blur. On automatic pilot, she followed the children from one activity to another, face painting followed by a balloon toss followed by more games. She somehow managed to get them to eat their lunch along the way.

Luckily for her, Riko seemed to be busy with his parents as soon as they arrived. He really was quite different when he was around the king and queen. He appeared stiffer, stood that much straighter.

Not that it was surprising. Parents or not, one had to demonstrate a certain level of decorum around a king and queen.

Glancing at him now across the square, her pulse skipped a beat. His head tilted in the king's direction, he was listening intently to whatever the other man was saying. Riko nodded in agreement to whatever it was he was hearing. Maybe they were discussing how disappointing it was that the Infanta Gina wasn't here. Was Riko disappointed that she hadn't made it? Had he been looking forward to spending time with her at such a fun event? She didn't want to think too long and hard about the potential answers.

Ramon ran over to her, distracting her from the disconcerting thoughts she had no business wondering about.

"This is my favorite song, Ms. Elle," he said, tugging at her pant leg. "Tatyana is dancing with Dad. Will you dance with me?"

She bowed to his height. "I would love to, young man."

The little boy thrust his hand in hers and led her to the makeshift dance floor. The bright afternoon was slowly giving way to a pleasant early evening with the stars faintly beginning to twinkle in the sky.

Elle walked with Ramon to the center of the throng of dancing bodies. The song was a fast and bouncy one. Some hip version of a Spanish pop song.

Ramon didn't so much as dance as hop from one foot to the other with a total disregard for the rhythm. His enthusiasm and energy were charmingly sweet, making Elle laugh at the sight of him.

Elle's gaze drifted over to the right of the stage where she'd last seen Riko with his parents. But the king and queen were the only ones there now. Her eyes scanned the periphery for him though she chastised herself for even wondering. She really had to find a way to stop thinking about the man.

At the next song, Tatyana came over to dance with them and the two children circled around her while trying to outdo each other with goofy moves.

Their antics had Elle laughing to the point of developing a cramp in her middle. She'd grown increasingly fond of them both in such a short span of time. It was going to be hard to walk away from the two of them when the time came.

The amusement suddenly faded and a sadness washed over her that she did her best to mask. It wasn't easy. She couldn't forget how temporary all this was. A year from now, her time spent on Versuvia would be a distant memory. This all may be a once in a lifetime experience for her, but she was nothing more than a blip in the life of the Suarez royal family. And that included Riko. Would he even remember her years from now? When he was crowned king and had a suitable wife as queen, how many thoughts would he give to the woman who'd pulled him onto the beach that fateful day then hired her to work at his family palace?

The odds were he wouldn't give her a passing thought. She was fooling herself if she thought otherwise.

Ramon suddenly stopped midswing, his attention focused on the distance toward the palace. Elle followed the direction of his gaze and saw what had drawn the little boy's attention.

"Mama!" he yelled, then made a beeline to where Manny was wheeling Isabel toward him. Tatyana was fast on his heels a moment later.

Just as well. Elle was suddenly feeling too melancholy to continue anyway.

But a hand on her arm stopped her before she could leave the dance floor. She looked up to find Riko had approached her when she hadn't been paying attention. He gave her a small bow then extended his other hand.

"May I?"

Riko knew he wasn't thinking straight. And that he was about to do something foolish and ill-advised. But he strode toward Elle on the dance floor, approaching her anyway. Today was about celebrating the kingdom. The only woman he wanted to celebrate with happened to be the one standing across him now. Watching her dance with the children had been an entertaining delight. All eyes had been on her. He would guess she probably had no idea.

She also probably didn't notice that no less than three men were getting ready to approach her to ask her to dance, including the staffer who had delivered her breakfast the other day. So Riko had made sure to beat them all to it. More than a few surprised gasps had reached his ears when he'd extended his hand to her.

He didn't much care. Right now, Riko's focus was solely on Elle. The garden lights had been turned on and they cast a golden hue that brought out the auburn highlights in her hair. Her eyes sparkled in the dimming light as the sun slowly began to set. He'd gone from amusement while watching her dance with Ramon to a sensation he didn't want to examine.

She still hadn't given him an answer. Wouldn't that be a gallon of fuel for the gossip mill if his kinsmen witnessed their crown prince being rejected for a casual dance.

Elle must have come to the same conclusion because she finally nodded reluctantly. "It would be an honor, Your Highness," she said before moving her feet to the beat of the song with zero enthusiasm. So, she was back to using his title. That didn't settle well in his gut. She couldn't honestly believe they could be so formal with each other. Not now. Too much had happened between them.

"The children are clearly enjoying your company," he said over the loud music. "Ramon doesn't often dance except with his mother or grandmother."

"I was just trying to keep up with him on the dance floor. Not sure how successful I was."

"It looked all good from where I was standing."

That was the absolute truth. The picture she'd made dancing and laughing with his little nephew on the dance floor was impossible to look away from. No wonder she'd garnered the attention of so many. The irritation and ire that attention drew from him shocked him in its intensity. Sebastian had been standing in the periphery of the dance floor, waiting to make his move, Riko was sure. The other man had made a step in Elle's direction as soon as the children left her side. Riko's need to intervene and stop him in his tracks had been both reflexive and powerful. There was no way he was going to let another man ask her to dance while he drew breath only a few feet away.

He knew he'd surprised his parents with the move. Well, he'd surprised himself as well.

A glance at his father across the way near the stage confirmed Riko's suspicions. His father looked beyond annoyed. So be it.

Elle followed his gaze. Astute as she was, she picked up on exactly what was happening. Not that the king's displeased expression as he watched his son was hard to read.

"Your father looks none too happy."

He wasn't. "We had a bit of a disagreement earlier, that's all. We will resolve it in due time."

He wasn't lying to her. The king made it clear that he thought Riko should have tried harder to reschedule Infanta Gina's visit, that he dropped the matter too easily and should have tried harder to have their respective people secure a set date rather than leave it up in the air.

But Riko had felt nothing but relief at the news that the Infanta Gina had matters to attend to in her country. He was able to enjoy the festival this way, not having to play tour guide and doting suitor to a woman he'd only met a handful of times.

Spending time in Elle's company instead.

"Are you sure that's the only reason?" she asked, her worried eyes still trained on the king.

Just like the other night on the veranda, he

found himself confiding in her once again. Stepping closer so he didn't need to shout over the noise, he leaned to speak into her ear. "He's disappointed Infanta Gina couldn't make it today."

Elle's eyebrows furrowed. "Surely he can't fault you for that. You told me it was a decision she made herself over a circumstance that couldn't be helped."

He shook his head. "You're right. What he's faulting me for is not trying harder to convince her how disappointed I am about the delay."

"I see," she answered, her lips tight. "And are you? Disappointed about not seeing her today?"

There was no way to answer that question without admitting much more than he was ready to tell her. So he simply shrugged. "She'll be here soon enough. It's only a postponement. My father is simply used to getting his own way and gets out of sorts when that doesn't happen."

"I see," she repeated, her voice so low that he had to strain to hear her.

For one insane moment, Riko had the urge to just take her by the hand and leave the floor with her. Leave the party altogether. He wanted her all to himself without a crowd of people around them.

And then he wanted to continue what they'd started when she'd fallen on him earlier today during that ridiculous race. How soft she'd felt everywhere their bodies touched. The taste of her lips, the pounding of her heart against his chest. He'd been thinking about that kiss ever since. Saints above, it had only served to whet his appetite. He wanted more from where that had come from.

And he desperately needed to know if she wanted the same. If Elle gave him the slightest indication that she may be interested in exploring something more, then Riko would do everything in his power to persuade his parents that he wasn't ready or willing to marry Gina.

He stopped any pretense of dancing and leaned in toward her. "I think I've had enough of the pounding music and big crowds for a while. Care to join me for a stroll in a much quieter area of the garden?"

She blinked up at him, worked her lips. "I don't think that's a good idea, Riko," she finally said after several beats.

A flood of disappointment rushed through his core. She couldn't mean because of the children; they were still with their parents. Looked like he had his answer, didn't he?

It was confirmed when she excused herself and walked away as soon as the song ended.

* * *

Riko watched Elle's back as she walked away toward the children. The party was in full swing, but he didn't feel much like partying anymore.

Was she simply skittish about pursuing a relationship? The other possibility had his blood pressure spiking. That she might be more interested in the staffer who had invited her to the beach party.

Well, he couldn't just stand out here staring after her. No doubt several eyes were on him right now. Besides, he could use a drink. He'd almost made it to the bar in the main sitting room before the deep baritone of his father's voice stopped him in his tracks. "Son, a word please."

He'd been so lost in thought, Riko hadn't even noticed that both his parents had been fast on his heels.

They entered the room somber-faced and tight-lipped. A palace staffer immediately appeared to wait on them before the king waved her away with a flick of his hand. The woman left, shutting the double doors firmly behind her. Clearly, she knew how to read a room.

His father didn't wait long to begin. "What in the devil's name are you thinking, son?"

Riko merely lifted an eyebrow.

His father was all too happy to clarify. "Why would you dance with your brother's nanny at all, let alone during such a public event?"

"It was one dance, Father. A silly one at that after the children left her standing on the dance floor." He would leave out the part about at least three other men waiting in the wings to pick up where Ramon and Tatyana had left off.

"So, you felt the need to fill the empty space on her dance card yourself? Is that it?"

Riko inhaled deeply. "If you noticed, Elle didn't stick around to do much dancing at all. She took off after the first song ended." A fact that still stung, he had to admit.

"Well, then, she's got more sense than you do. What are we supposed to tell our press office to say when they're asked about this?" his father demanded to know.

Riko shrugged. "Tell them that Elle and I are friends. I enjoy her company."

The king visibly bristled. "We will absolutely not be telling them that last part. The only woman whose company you should be entertaining is the infanta."

Riko almost chuckled at how ridiculous that sounded. Somehow, he managed to keep it suppressed. "It was just a dance, Father. Nothing more."

His father rubbed a hand down his face, his

expression so weary, Riko almost felt the need to apologize. Almost.

"If it makes things any better, I don't foresee any more dancing in Elle's and my future."

His father's features softened ever so slightly. "See that there isn't."

"Yes, sir," Riko assured him, not that it had been his decision in the least. With a respectful bow to each parent, he turned and left the room.

He wasn't surprised when the queen caught up with him a few short moments later in the main hallway. His mother had appeared to be holding back what she'd wanted to say during the king's tirade.

"Son, wait."

Riko closed his eyes before turning to face her, doing his best to summon some of his swiftly dwindling patience. "Yes, Mother?"

She turned to look over her shoulder, as if to make sure no one else was in the vicinity. There was no one. They were alone. So why the cautious glance?

"I'd like you to consider something," she told Riko, turning back to face him.

"What's that?"

"Your father isn't getting any younger. Neither of us are. Please keep that in mind as you follow your impulses."

Impulses. Was that really how she was going to refer to his attempts at having some say in the direction his life might take? "What does that mean exactly, Mother?"

She tilted her head, as if disappointed with his question. "It means he's not the young, energetic man who inherited the throne decades ago. He tires more easily. He needs more rest."

He studied his mother's face. The concern there was unmistakable. "He's not a young man any longer," she added.

Riko pinched the bridge of his nose. "Point taken, Mother. I understand."

She lifted her chin as she studied him. "I hope you do."

With that, the queen spun on her heel and walked back toward the king and queen's wing.

Riko watched her for several beats before making his way back to his own wing, his thoughts even murkier than they'd been just moments ago.

There had to be some kind of mistake. Elle just knew it couldn't be morning yet. She'd only just crawled into bed and shut her eyes. Unlike the insomnia-laden hours of her first night at the palace, she'd been out as soon as her head had hit the pillow. A physically tiring and emotionally exhausting day could do that to a girl, she supposed.

On one hand, she should be surprised that her insomnia seemed to have cured itself. On the other, the same thoughts and images had still managed to invade her dreams. Not surprisingly, they all involved one charming and handsome prince she couldn't erase from her mind even during sleep.

Pictures from the previous day ran through her mind like a slideshow. Dancing with Riko. His arms around her as she fell. The touch of his lips softly brushing against hers. Heaven help her, she could still taste him now over the mint from her nightly toothpaste.

What was wrong with her? How had she ended up in such a position? Pining after a man, thinking of him nonstop. It just wasn't like her. She'd had her share of crushes, had dated a couple of men regularly. None of them had lasted long. She couldn't recall ever actually feeling as if she might be falling for someone.

Just her luck that the first time she had those feelings, they had to be for a man who was so far out of her reach he might as well be in another stratosphere.

A crown prince. One who was supposed to

be entertaining an infanta he might become engaged to.

She groaned as she thought of the way she'd asked him point-blank whether he was disappointed that Gina's arrival had been delayed. What had possessed her to do such a thing? Riko hadn't given her any kind of answer. Which was answer enough in itself, wasn't it? He really was ready to marry the infanta. A woman much more fitting for him given his station in life. Elle would be fooling herself to think otherwise for even a moment.

With another groan of frustration, she reached for her phone where it was charging on the bedside table. Her screen was covered in message alerts when she lifted it. All from her sisters. All said different versions of essentially the same thing.

…saw you online…

…dancing in front of a grand palace…

…an actual prince!

There'd been photographers at the festivities yesterday, plenty of them. She hadn't realized that she'd been the subject of any photographs. Elle felt a jolt of panic spark through her as the thought crossed her mind. Had a photo been taken when she and Riko had been on the ground, during the ever so brief moment when he'd kissed her?

She inhaled a deep breath and aimed for some calm. Surely not, or her sisters would have most certainly led with that. Scrolling through the rest, she was further relieved that no mention was made of any such thing.

The relief was short-lived. At the bottom was a message that was much more serious and much more crushing. Her father.

Are you really over in Europe to babysit, Elle? Isn't it time to come home and begin working toward a real future?

A blanket of weariness settled over her at the words on her screen. Her father was actually referring to her highly appreciated, so far genuinely rewarding, new nanny position as if she were a teenager looking for pocket money hired to watch a couple of toddlers during their parents' date night.

Well, he might be a brilliant and successful man, but in this case he was wrong. Elle already adored Tatyana and Ramon. Manny and Isabel had made her feel more like a family friend than an employee since she'd arrived.

She was responsible for making sure the children did their studies, ate at their scheduled times, and were entertained and safe in her care. So much more than simply babysitting. Of course, her father would never see it that way, even if she bothered trying to explain. The two of them didn't often see eye to eye on much, if anything.

She didn't have it in her to reply to him. What would she even say? Or to her sisters for that matter.

Reluctantly, she got out of bed though it was so tempting to crawl back under the covers and hit the snooze button. But that was a slippery slope. And she didn't want to be late for the second day of the National Spirit Festival.

Another alert sounded on her phone just as she was done showering. Worried that it might be her father again to drive his point home, or her mother this time, Elle hesitated. But it was Isabel's contact info that appeared on her screen when she glanced at it. A text requesting to meet with her before she gathered the children from their breakfast.

Curiosity piqued, Elle made her way to Manny and Isabel's wing. The princess lay reclined on her bed again this morning when Elle entered the room.

"Good morning, Elle," she said, greeting her

with a warm, friendly smile. "I hope you slept well."

"Like a brick," Elle answered.

Isabel blinked at her in confusion.

"Sorry. It's an American idiom that doesn't translate well."

"Hmm." She patted the mattress next to her. "Come sit, dear. There's something I need to run by you."

"What is it?" Elle asked, sitting on the bed.

"Part of the celebrations tomorrow evening involve a symphony concert followed by a rather formal dinner."

"That sounds lovely. How will the children be participating?"

"That's just it. They won't be. The concert is rather late, past their bedtime."

Sounded like she might be about to get the evening off. Which should have been welcome. But Elle wasn't sure what she'd do with herself.

But Isabel's next words threw her for a loop. "With the absence of Infanta Gina, there'll be an empty chair in the box and an uneven number at the table. It just won't do given how many pictures are taken at these things."

Elle merely nodded, not sure what any of this might have to do with her.

"I was wondering if you might attend both events. Just to sort of fill in."

It was Elle's turn to be surprised. "Me? I don't understand."

Isabel smiled at her. "Well, I simply don't have the time or energy to try to come up with a replacement for the infanta at this stage. And Manny is of absolutely no help. And such mundane matters are beneath the king and queen."

Elle stammered for a way to respond. She was certain to feel and look out of place. But the concept of attending royal events as an actual guest seemed like a once in a lifetime opportunity too good to pass up. On the other hand, what if she made a fool of herself by using the wrong fork or something?

"Would you like to attend then, Elle?" Isabel asked. "I know it's short notice, but the schedule really has gotten rather chaotic given the change." She glanced outside the window. The sky was gray and covered in rolling clouds. "And it looks like we're going to have to postpone today's festivities given the weather. Just adding more overall chaos."

Elle swallowed through the confusion causing a rocklike lump in her throat when Isabel delivered the coup de grâce. "Consider it a favor to me."

How in the world would she say no to that? One didn't simply turn down such a request from a princess.

"It would be an honor," she told her. "Thank you for thinking to ask me."

"Well, if I'm to be honest, I should tell you that it wasn't originally my idea."

"Oh?"

Isabel shook her head. "I must admit that it was Riko's idea."

Elle tried to hide her reaction at that bit of news. Riko had been the one to think of her?

"Huh."

"That's right. He mentioned you've been pursuing a career in music before being waylaid for a while. He thought a concert would be something you might enjoy."

Elle's mouth went dry. "How very kind of him. I will have to thank him first chance I get."

CHAPTER NINE

ELLE STEPPED BACK into her room to try and regroup before going to get the children for the day. She was still processing what had just happened and exactly how she felt about it.

The morning had grown even darker on her way back, casting shadows over the walls and furniture. It had been Riko's idea to invite her. She didn't dare look too far into that. She'd simply been the easiest choice—free for the evening and already residing at the palace. Thoughts of Riko brought other questions to mind. Like how good would the man look in a tuxedo? Would they be sitting anywhere close to each other at the concert? Or at dinner?

Her phone dinged. Her sister Lizzie again.

Are you there? You've gone silent and we are dying of curiosity back home.

She'd added several sad face emojis at the end. This time Elle began to answer back. Wait till her sisters heard about her invitation to attend a concert and a formal dinner with the royal family.

Lizzie picked up on the first ring.

Elle breathlessly answered her myriad questions then told her about the morning's conversation with Isabel.

Lizzie actually squealed. "How exciting, Elle! What do you think you'll wear?"

Elle jolted at the question. How could that have not even occurred to her? Leave it to her logical, pragmatic, state's attorney sister to immediately bring it up. "Lizzie, I'll have to call you back," she said into the phone then began to pace after hanging up.

There was nothing in her closet that would even remotely suffice. In fact, she'd actually felt underdressed at even the casual activities she'd been to so far at the castle. Were there boutiques near the palace? Surely they wouldn't be within walking distance. Who would she ask for a ride?

She was loath to ask Riko, further cementing her out of place status in his eyes. And she didn't want to bother Isabel; the woman had enough to deal with.

A ringing sound interrupted her panicked thoughts. The landline phone that hung on the wall near the door. It had to be some kind of internal palace communication system. Elle hadn't really noticed it until this very moment.

Curious about who would try to contact her in such a way, she went to answer it. A woman with an accent responded when she said hello.

"Hello, miss. I am just calling to schedule your fitting."

"Fitting?"

"Yes, miss. Would this afternoon work for your schedule? Say around one?"

That was right around the time the children sat down for their lunch with their parents. Which would leave her free. "Yes. Thank you. That would be fine."

Elle stared at the receiver as she replaced it. Had she just gotten a solution to her wardrobe problem?

Four hours later, after a hectic and busy morning with the children, Elle got her answer when a knock sounded on her door.

She opened it to find a short, smiling woman in a smart business suit and sensible heels.

"Hello, I am Seema. Are you ready?"

Elle couldn't be sure. But she stepped aside to let the woman in then gasped in surprise when she realized Seema wasn't alone. Two men walked in behind her wheeling several racks full of clothing. A third man walked in carrying a large boxy briefcase.

They deposited the items in the middle of the room then left, shutting the door behind them.

Elle didn't know what hit her. The next ninety minutes passed by in a flurry of fittings and slipping in and out of shoes. Seema was friendly and personable, making the experience less daunting and nerve-racking than it otherwise might have been.

"Eight hours ago, I had no idea I'd even be attending such an event," she found herself admitting to Seema. "I'm invited only because there's an open chair due to the infanta's unexpected absence."

"Nature hates a vacuum. And so does the royal family," Seema quipped as she pinned yet another spot on the dress she currently wore.

"There," the other woman said, stepping back to look Elle over. "I believe this is the one."

Elle summoned the courage to turn and look at herself in the mirror. Her breath caught at the image. Was that really her? She was draped in a silky dress of emerald green that brought out the fiery red shade of her hair and accented the hazel in her eyes. She looked like she might even be an actual princess herself.

Oh, Seema was so very right. The dress was indeed the one.

✦ ✦ ✦

Riko ran up the main stairway to the staff residence hallway, a million and one thoughts scrambling through his head. He normally resented having to attend symphony concerts, the music much too slow and stuffy for his liking. And the formal dinners afterward were always such a strained bore of a time. The two events were really the only part of the National Spirit Festival week that Riko didn't enjoy.

But tonight, he found himself looking forward to both activities. There was only one reason for that. And that reason would be the woman who was to be his unofficial date tonight.

When he knocked on her door minutes later, she opened it within a heartbeat. But then his heart almost stopped when took in the sight of her.

The dress she wore was the color of the emerald jewels that glimmered on the royal crown and crest. Her hair was done up in some complicated style and shimmered with thin strands of some kind of glittery thread. The strapless dress showed off her elegant shoulders and the arch of her delicate neck. And heaven help him, it clung to her in all the right places. She looked like a vision out of a skilled painter's masterpiece.

"Elle?" He didn't even know why he'd said her name like a question. His mind wasn't working straight. He couldn't even think, could barely breathe.

"Good evening, Riko," she said. Even her voice sounded different. Smoother, softer, like a light breeze floating to his ears.

She glanced up and down the hallway.

"Apologies. I didn't get a chance to notify you. I'll be accompanying you in the car on the way to the symphony."

Her lips tightened and a rosy spot of color appeared on her cheeks. "I see. What about the others?"

"Just us in the car. The king and queen have to make a formal entrance, of course. And Isabel needed more time. They'll join us shortly."

Elle looked off to the side. Was she dreading his company then? Why was she apprehensive that the two of them would be alone for the duration of the ride? It vexed him that he couldn't read her.

He offered her his elbow when she stepped into the hallway and led her down the marble staircase unsure what to say. His head was still spinning, in shock at the vision Elle made on his arm. In a true grasp at cliché, he settled on the weather. "I must apologize for all this rain when you're dressed so sharply."

She chuckled before answering. "You can hardly be blamed for the weather, Riko. Even you don't wield that kind of command."

She thought him commanding? The idea pleased him more than was logical.

When they reached the main doors, two guards appeared at either side with umbrellas to ward off the rain that had started this morning and lasted throughout the whole day. The day might have been a bust with all the planned outdoor activities being postponed, but this evening was starting off quite to his liking.

One of the official limousines with the royal Suarez crest on the hood sat waiting at the bottom of the steps.

He led Elle with a hand to the small of her back, the skin on his palm tingling at the contact point. His whole body was strumming. A staffer held the door of the stretch limousine open for them, and he guided her inside before joining her in the seat. His heart skipped as his thigh brushed against her silk-clad one.

"The children were awfully disappointed that today's festivities had to be moved to the rain date in a couple days," she said.

"I can't say I blame them. Today would have been the much anticipated kayak races along the river."

"Yes, they mentioned it more than once."

Riko barely heard what she'd said, his attention drifting to the way her hair glimmered from the soft blue glow of the roof lights. He couldn't help but let his gaze wander from the top of her magnificent head to the tips of her painted toes.

Since when had he been the type of man to appreciate a woman's toes?

He gave his head a shake and looked up to find her eyes on him. Great. He'd been caught ogling her like some sort of lovesick teenager. Her hand drifted up to the back of her neck and then to her chest.

"Is something wrong? Is this dress okay? It isn't my usual style, but I wanted to try something different. I'm terribly sorry if it's not working for the evening that's planned."

Riko blinked at her. Was she really apologizing because she thought she wasn't dressed right? How could she even consider the possibility?

He shook his head ever so slowly. "Believe me, Elle. The dress is more than just okay. You look incredible." He figured he should stop there. If he continued, he seriously ran the risk of overcomplimenting her and stammering his praise like the aforementioned teenager.

She swallowed. "You're sure? I probably

should have asked Isabel before making a choice. I just don't want to intrude on her too often as she's resting."

"Trust me. You didn't need to confer with anyone. The choice of dress is perfect for tonight."

In his eyes, Elle herself was perfect. A knowledge that was becoming increasingly harder to deny.

She'd stepped into a fairy tale. Complete with a dreamy prince.

Elle watched the glowing lights of the kingdom below as they drove away from the palace and along the winding road that meandered down the mountain.

How was any of this happening? To her, Arielle Stanton of Chicago, Illinois? To think, it had all started during a storm much like this one. From this day on, she would consider stormy days lucky and never complain about lightning or rain or thunder. Then she felt guilty for even thinking that first storm was good luck in any way because of the danger Riko had been in. Lucky or not, it had brought the two of them to this very moment.

The shock of finding Riko at her door announcing that he'd be accompanying her personally had yet to wear off. It didn't help that the man looked like temptation in physical form the way he wore the tuxedo that had clearly been tailored to fit him to a tee.

When they arrived at the concert hall and Riko walked her through the grand lobby and up to the balcony, pretending to be a princess was becoming all too easy.

"I haven't thanked you yet for agreeing to come tonight," Riko said once they'd taken their seats.

Elle had to stifle a laugh at that comment. She should be the one thanking him.

He glanced at the gold watch on his wrist. "The concert should be over in under two hours or so."

She didn't hide her chuckle this time. "It hasn't even started yet. And I'm looking forward to it."

"That's where we differ. I'm looking forward to it being over."

"Not a fan of classical music, I take it?"

He shook his head. "Probably due to all the hours of violin I was made to practice as a child. All I wanted to do was run around outside or at least study an instrument a bit more exciting."

"Like what?"

He shrugged. "The drums maybe. Or guitar. Electric preferably. Maybe even the tuba."

Elle's laughter grew and she clamped a hand to her mouth. The people already assembled in the seats below didn't seem the type to giggle their way into an auditorium. "Somehow I can't picture you roaming around the palace blowing on a tuba."

"Neither could my mother and father. I was told any prince worth his salt had to master a classical instrument. No one seemed able to tell me why. Especially considering Manny was allowed to try his hand at the ukulele of all things."

It occurred to her just how different the lives of the two princes had been. By a twist of fate that had literally amounted to minutes.

Not all that different from her upbringing with her sisters. Elle wasn't the only daughter in the family with a singing voice. But while her sisters had only sung recreationally or for school plays, Elle was the only one who insisted on training her voice in the hopes of a vocal career someday.

"I wasn't given the opportunity to study what I wanted until I reached the age when I could pursue it on my own."

He laid his hand over hers. "Your singing."

So he had been listening to her that night on the veranda. And he did remember what she'd told him. "That's right. Mom and Dad absolutely refused to pay for any kind of singing lessons."

"So you can sing and you're a great swimmer. Quite the talented young woman."

It was going to be hard not to let his compliments go to her head.

She explained the history behind her abilities in the water. "We lived near Lake Michigan, so the water was my refuge when I needed to get away from all the structure and rules rampant in my house. I would take every opportunity to swim in the summer. During the colder months, I found any indoor pool there was until I could jump into the lake again. It made sense to join the swim team in high school when the time came."

"Lucky for me," Riko said. "Though I wish I could remember more precisely how you saved me that day."

It hardly mattered whether he did or not given all that had transpired since. "Who knows. Maybe you will someday," she answered.

"Hopefully. And who knows, maybe someday I can pick up the electric guitar," he said, though didn't sound convinced of his statement at all. Then he grunted a laugh. "Can you imagine?" Riko added after a beat, amusement laced in his voice. "A ukulele."

She could. Her imagination was in full

force, actually. For instance, just for tonight, she wanted to pretend that the fairy tale she'd stepped into could somehow be real. That she was here as part of this life. A part of Riko's world in truth. Not because she was filling in for the woman who rightfully should be here.

What would be the harm in that?

The nagging voice inside her head told her exactly how damaging such dreaming might be. For her heart. She had to believe the memories alone would be worth it.

Isabel and Manny arrived not long after. Manny wheeled his wife to the row behind them. He gave Elle an appraising look and blew out a whistle of appreciation. "Wow. Elle, you clean up good."

The comment earned him a chuckle from his wife and a glare from Riko.

A commotion from her left drew her attention and Riko clasped her hand, signaling her to rise as he did. Manny stood as well while Isabel bowed her head. The king and queen had arrived and were settling into their seats in an adjacent balcony. She remained standing with the two brothers until their parents sat down.

The lights began to dim lower and lower but not before Elle stole a glance at the royal couple to catch a clearly displeased expression on the king's face as he looked upon his heir.

Surprisingly, his look of disapproval didn't upset her as much as it perhaps should have. For all their differences, maybe she and Riko actually did have some similarities.

After all, she was familiar with such looks. Her father's icy cold glare could give the Versuvian king a run for his money.

CHAPTER TEN

RIKO SHOULD HAVE checked the seating arrangements before dinner started. To his disappointment, Elle wasn't seated anywhere near him. Of course, he was seated to the right of his father with his mother two chairs away next to his father. Would it have been too much to ask that Elle be seated on his other side. Instead, it was one of the kingdom's economic ministers who was probably going to talk his ear off about the European markets, which was boring enough under normal circumstances. Tonight would be much worse given how distracted Riko was. He didn't think he could even feign indifference the way he normally did with the man.

He watched her now at the other end of the table. She was sitting next to one of the country's top journalists and apparently he was telling her something very interesting based on the way she kept nodding and smiling at the man. He had a ridiculous urge to walk over there and ask the reporter to switch chairs with him. He almost laughed out loud at that suggestion. He could just imagine how that might go over with the king and queen.

"Do you have time in your schedule first thing tomorrow to do that, son?" he heard his father ask as the first course of garden salad and fresh rolls was brought out by the wait staff.

Do what? Riko hadn't heard his father speak let alone knew what question he was being asked. He scrambled to come up with a generic answer that might cover a wide range of the king's asks, but his father was on to him. He grunted with displeasure. "You're not even listening to me, are you?"

Riko pinched the bridge of his nose. "I apologize, Father. It has been a rather long day. And I'm afraid I have a slew of emails to answer and calls to make upon our return to the castle."

The king tore apart one of the dinner rolls as if it had caused him injury and then dropped it on his place without even taking a bite. "Perhaps one of those calls could be to the infanta?"

Riko tried not to physically react to the suggestion. The truth was, he'd forgotten all about

Infanta Gina and her as yet not rescheduled visit.

"What would you have me say to her, Your Highness?" Mistake. Riko should have simply answered in the affirmative and worried about it tomorrow. Now he was going to get an earful.

The king lowered his fork, which had been about to spear a slice of tomato in his salad. "I can write you a script, son. But I think the gist of it should be that you inquire how she's doing and remind her she has an invitation to Palacio Suarez which we hope she will honor within the next day or so."

His mother leaned over to join the conversation. "Better yet, maybe he should be the one to go visit her."

Not going to happen. He had to stop this train in its tracks. The only way Riko could think to do that was to agree to the original ask. "I'll be certain to call her first thing tomorrow." As loath as he was to give so much as an inch, he hoped that would be the end of the conversation. No such luck.

His father went on, "Be sure to tell her that we all await her visit with great anticipation."

Riko merely nodded at that, unwilling to lie to his father outright. His attention drifted back to Elle's end of the table. She hadn't so much as glanced in his direction. Could the journalist really be that interesting? He willed her to look up at him, to offer him that fetching smile of hers he'd gotten so used to brightening up his days and that floated through his mind at night.

His salad was untouched still when the next course arrived, chilled seafood with an array of dipping sauces. Elle smiled at the waiter when her plate was delivered, the server lingering just a little too long after he'd set the plate down.

Riko swore inside and rubbed a hand down his face. He couldn't very well get annoyed with every man who so much as made eye contact with her. Besides, he could take solace in the fact that he'd be the one sitting next to her in the car later, the one walking her up the stairs of the palace and to her room.

It hit him like a thunderbolt. Oh, man. He had it bad. He was falling for her. Hard. What a completely inappropriate and utterly messy fiasco. He was expected to make a match that would bring gains to the kingdom. His parents had made their decision already about who that match should be with. But he felt nothing for the infanta. Whereas simply seeing Elle made his pulse quicken and his heart race. And his attraction wasn't like some kind of faucet he could turn on and off.

It was as if his father sensed the dangerous direction his thoughts had taken. He leaned over to Riko, close enough that their shoulders were touching. "I'd like to make something very clear, son," he said softly. The timbre and tone of his voice left no doubt that Riko was being addressed by King Guillermo, honored monarch of Versuvia. Not his father.

Riko cleared his throat. "What's that, sir?" he asked, though he could guess.

"I'll be forever grateful to the young lady for coming to your aid after the boating accident. But my indulgence only goes so far."

Message received. Loud and clear.

The only question was, was Riko willing to heed it?

Elle knew this fairy-tale night was coming to an end. No amount of wishing would change that.

But she was so not ready to have the magic stop. The long black limo pulled up in front of the palace doors, and a footman appeared immediately to open her door. But Riko was the one who took her by the hand and helped her out of the car.

He led her up the steps and through the

foyer, his palm resting gently on the small of her back. Such an innocent touch. But it was setting her on fire inside. She'd been trying so hard not to stare at him all night. It hadn't been easy, but she knew if he caught her looking at him with all the emotions churning in her chest, there would be no hiding the attraction she felt for him.

"I hope you had a good time, *cariña*," he said now when they made it to her hallway and down to her door.

The last word dripped from his mouth like honey. That was the second time he'd called her that, and it made her muscles turn to goo.

There were no words for her to answer that question fairly.

"I had a lovely time. I must thank your family for including me first chance I get. And I'll have to thank Isabel for sending the seamstress to make sure I had something fitting to wear."

Riko looked off to the side. "I don't think you need to mention it. I'm sure she was happy to do it."

Something in the tone of his voice and the way he wasn't making eye contact had her suspicions rising. Then she put two and two together. "It was you, wasn't it? You're the one who sent Seema up to see me."

He ducked his head. "Guilty as charged."

Elle was beyond touched at his consideration for her to even think of such a thing let alone making it happen. "Thank you, Riko. Really. That was very kind of you."

"It was more than worthwhile. You looked breathtaking. The most alluring woman there."

Her heart was about to pound out of her chest at his words and the way he was looking at her. That settled it. There was no way she was going to let him walk away and leave her alone just yet.

"If you're not tired," she began, "this is usually the time of night I sit out on my balcony just to stare at the night sky."

Riko leaned his shoulder up against the door frame, bringing his body that much closer to hers. "Are you asking me to join you?"

"Yes," she answered, still not quite believing that she was being bold enough to do just that.

"I'd love to."

She walked through the door and switched the light on. Soft yellow light from the small crystal chandelier washed over the room. Making her way to the balcony, she pulled the double doors open and stepped out. Riko followed behind her.

It might have been a scene out of a movie. Her standing there under the starlit sky, wearing a dress made for a princess, a handsome tuxedoed prince standing behind her. But Riko wasn't just a royal heir. He was charismatic beyond measure. So affectionate that his small niece and nephew appeared to adore him. And considerate enough to make sure that an unprepared nanny was fitted with a dress.

How in the world was she not to fall in love with him?

She heard a rustling behind her and turned to find he'd slipped off his jacket and unbuttoned the top three buttons of his shirt. He proceeded to roll up his sleeves, and her breath caught at the masculine, devastatingly handsome figure he posed. She knew it was, oh, so dangerous for her to be out here alone with him given where her emotions were leading her. But there was no turning back now. She was way past the point of no return.

"It's a beautiful night," he said, casually striding over to where she stood behind the railing. Then he leaned his forearms on the steel bar, so close, her thigh brushed against his hip and sent a bolt of electricity through her limb.

He was right. The diamond-bright twinkling stars above, the crisp post-rain night air, the slight scent of the ocean in the distance made for a spectacular potpourri for the senses.

But she could hardly pay attention to any of it.

Her sole focus was Riko and the currents of longing running through every inch of her body.

"I'm sorry we didn't get a chance to sit together at dinner," he told her. "I didn't think to check the seating arrangements beforehand."

She'd been sorry about that too. Had spent most of the meal wishing he was closer. "That's all right. I understand you had to sit next to your parents. And my seatmates were nice enough."

He continued to stare at the horizon. "Nice, huh? The one gentleman appeared to be talking your ear off."

Did she detect a note of jealousy? "I hardly heard a word he was saying."

He straightened then, turned to face her and stepped even closer. She could feel his breath hot against her cheek, his now familiar scent filling her senses. "Why's that?"

She tilted her head, studying him through the dark shadows the full moon was casting on his face. "Why all the questions about my dinner conversation?"

His eyes darkened. "Because all night I wanted to leap across the table and pull the man out of his chair to take his place beside you," he bit out, his voice full of frustration. "It took all the restraint I had not to do just that."

Elle had to fight for her next breath. "Riko." His name escaped her lips on a soft whisper, her hand reaching for him when she didn't even know she'd lifted it.

The next instant his lips were on hers, his arms wrapped tight around her. His hand traveled lower behind her back until he was cupping her bottom and pulling her even tighter against his length. The contours of his chest pressed deliciously against her skin. The world stopped—she was convinced her heart had stopped. Nothing else mattered but this man and the way he tasted on her lips. She dragged her hands over his shoulders, thrust her fingers through the thick curls of hair above his neck.

She'd been dreaming of this moment, yearning for it. Still, she wasn't prepared for the sensations Riko's kiss evoked.

Nothing could have prepared her.

He was going to need much more coffee than his usual espresso. Riko was useless this morning and finally shut his laptop cover and leaned back in his office chair, swiveling it around to look out the three-panel bay window that overlooked the elaborate maze in the South Garden. Unlike the rain yesterday, the weather this morning matched his mood to a tee. Bright and sunny, the horizon an aqua blue.

Kissing Elle last night had literally knocked the wind out of him, taking a good portion of the night to get his breathing back to normal. He'd actually needed a cold shower.

He'd wanted to spend the night in that small room with her more than he'd wanted his next breath. But as a gentleman, when a clear and direct invitation hadn't been extended, he'd left her on the balcony after another lingering kiss.

All the pity.

Now, he couldn't wait to kiss her again. See where it might lead this time.

First, he would have the conversation with his parents that he'd been dreading. There was no putting it off any longer. Though it was too late to cancel the infanta's visit without causing an international scandal, he had to make clear to the king and queen that no match would be made. His feelings for Elle had simply grown too strong to ignore.

He glanced at this watch. She'd be gathering the children right about now after their breakfast.

An incoming call required his attention and he clicked the answer icon, only glancing at the screen afterward to see it was Gina on the other end of the line.

He had to stifle a groan.

"Riko!" she said breathlessly through the small speaker, as if she might be in motion. Riko got a squirmy feeling in the pit of his stomach when he thought of what that might mean. "Good news," Gina added. "I'm on my way. Finally! I'll be landing in Versuvia in a couple short hours."

Riko swore under his breath. He'd been right. Gina went on talking. He could hardly concentrate on what she was saying through the panic pounding through his veins. "I'm sorry I didn't go through official channels to announce my travel plans, but when the opportunity came, I just jumped to get started on the journey."

"That's…uh…that's great news. I'm glad to hear it." That might have been the biggest lie he'd ever told in his life. But what was the alternative? He couldn't very well tell the woman not to come, over the phone no less. The international chaos storm insulting the infanta would cause would be monumental and instantaneous. Political strain between the two nations was the last thing anyone needed.

"Isn't this a relief?" she asked, chuckling. "Bet you were worried I'd never get there."

How far from the target she was. "Of course," he lied again.

"I'll text your office the details."

He thanked her, knowing just how stiff he sounded, but his mind was racing with all that this development meant for him.

And for Elle.

"I'll be sure to have them arrange for an official greeting when you land on Versuvian soil," he told her.

"Lovely. Goodbye until we see each other, then."

"Goodbye," Riko replied, ending the call. Then he threw his phone across the room against the wall so hard that the corner of the screen cracked and dislodged a portion of the wall's plaster.

His brother chose that moment to enter the room. Without knocking, of course.

"Not now, Manny. I have a colossal mess on my hands. The infanta just called me personally to announce she'll be arriving in Versuvia before lunch."

"And that's a problem? I thought we were expecting her at some point."

Riko gave him a pointed look. They were twins, had spent their entire lives together. He waited for Manny to figure it out.

It took only a second. "Ah, I see. A certain red-haired former mermaid who happens to be under this roof reading to my children at the moment."

Riko thrust his hands through his hair.

Manny shut the door and strode into the room. "I mean I kind of surmised where your head was at when it came to Elle. But I guess I didn't realize the full extent of the...complication."

"Don't use that word."

Manny shrugged. "No other way to put it, big brother."

He was right, as much as it pained Riko to admit it. Things had gotten unfathomably complicated. He would have to get through the next forty-eight hours performing a balancing act where he treated Gina with the utmost respect and consideration while not giving her the wrong idea about his attraction to her. Or lack thereof.

And there was Elle. "I have to figure out what to tell her."

"Well, you should figure it out soon."

"What do you mean?"

Manny's eyes narrowed on him. "You really aren't yourself, are you?"

What the devil was he talking about? Riko made a circular motion with his hand in a gesture of "come out with it."

"If you were thinking straight, you'd realize that as she was calling you, her office was probably calling the king's staff to officially announce her arrival."

Riko bit out another curse. He was right, again.

Manny continued. "Which means..." He didn't need to finish.

Riko finished for him. "Which means the announcement is traveling through all the family members as we speak so that they may prepare to greet her."

Which in turn meant that Isabel would need to have the children ready for the visit as well.

Riko didn't bother to say goodbye to his brother. He wordlessly walked by him and half jogged, half walked to the children's nursery.

He burst in without bothering to knock. The children cheered with delight when they saw him.

But Elle's reaction to his entrance was anything but cheerful.

He was too late.

Elle wanted to kick herself. Because the first reaction she'd had when Riko burst through the door wasn't one of anger, or frustration. No. Rather it was a tugging in the area of her heart at seeing him for the first time since their passionate kisses last night.

At least she'd quickly recovered.

Enough to turn him down when he asked his question after patting the heads of both the children. "I know you're on duty. But can we go to the corner of the room and talk for a minute?"

She shook her head. "I'm afraid I can't. I have to get the children properly dressed and ready. I've just received a notification text that they are to be greeting a VIP this afternoon." Imagine her surprise when she'd gotten that text. Riko hadn't made any mention of Infanta Gina yesterday. He could have given her the courtesy of a warning at the least. Had he merely been toying with her last night? It was the only explanation that made sense.

"Elle—"

She cut him off. She really didn't have the emotional fortitude for this conversation right now. "This isn't the time or place."

His lips thinned into a tight line. "Fine, but we'll need to talk at some point."

Tatyana must have sensed the tension in the air despite her age. She ran over and hugged her uncle's leg. Riko immediately dropped to her level and gave her a reassuring smile.

Heat rose to Elle's cheeks as she watched him with the child, remembering the taste of his kisses on the balcony just a night ago. The way he'd looked at her with hunger flooding his eyes. How quickly things could change.

It had taken all her willpower last night to

refrain from asking him to stay, to spend the night with her on the bed just a few feet away.

Thank the heavens above she hadn't done so. Imagining how much worse all this would feel if they'd actually been intimate had her shuddering inside.

Considering how shattering simply kissing him had been, she would never have recovered.

She probably never would anyway.

CHAPTER ELEVEN

THE WOMAN WAS everything Elle had imagined she would be. Elegant, graceful, charming and so very regal. A woman fit to marry a prince and serve as queen when he inherited the throne. Infanta Gina appeared to have been born and bred for just that purpose.

She had sparkling blue eyes and hair the color of spun gold. Exactly the way storybooks described so many fictional queens. She wore a smart navy blue suit and sensible matching pumps the exact same shade. Her shoes alone were probably worth more than the house Elle had grown up in.

Elle stood rod straight in the corner of the great hall, in a line with other staff members, as she was greeted by the royal family. She watched the scene unfold with a fake smile pasted on her face. She'd been careful to apply the correct mask and was doing her best to keep it in place.

Riko's glance kept darting in Elle's direction,

but she made sure to keep her eyes averted.
What was he expecting from her? A friendly
smile? A flirtatious wink?

He'd called her repeatedly since this morning, but she hadn't had it in her to pick up, finally resorting to text messages.

You have to realize I didn't know.

Elle wasn't sure what she was supposed to
do with that bit of information. It hardly made
a difference to what she was experiencing right
now, did it?

She scanned the room, glancing at anyone
but Riko. When her gaze fell on Manny, she
was surprised to find that he'd been watching
her. He flashed her a kind smile. Elle paused,
not sure how she felt about the sympathy. Did
he know? Or was it because her mask wasn't
working as well as she would like to think?

Not that it made any difference.

The last in line for introductions were Ramon
and Tatyana. They each performed excellent
curtsies until Tatyana took it too far and nearly
toppled over. Elle would have to make sure to
hug the little girl later for providing at least a
sliver of lightheartedness to the otherwise miserable experience. Thank the spirits for the both
of them. Ramon and Tatyana had kept her busy

and distracted throughout the day leading up to this miserable moment. Well, as distracted as was possible.

Just when she thought the little discomfort was over and she could unclench her jaw, Riko and the infanta turned to the corner where Elle stood with the others. To her horror, they both approached.

"And this is our household staff you might be interacting with during your stay," Riko said, his gaze square on Elle's.

A brick dropped into her throat. She was going to be introduced to the infanta also? Why had no one told her? How in the world was she supposed to react?

How stupid of her not have figured it out. There had to be a reason she and the rest of the staff were here, after all.

As luck would have it, she was last in line. At least she had some examples to follow. Each of the staffers before her bowed and welcomed the woman. She replied with a thanks and a smile to each.

When at last it came time for her turn, Elle managed the bow just fine. But when she went to speak the words of welcome, the brick had lodged itself fully at the base of her throat.

The words refused to come out. She'd completely lost her voice.

* * *

Riko was beginning to get tired of playing Prince Charming. Especially considering the way his mind kept wandering when he was supposed to be listening intently to Gina. Not very charming of him.

They were strolling through the Suarez gardens trailing the king and queen. His mother had decided to join them under the pretense of wanting fresh air, but Riko could guess her true motive. She was doing her best to strain and hear their conversation. So Riko kept falling farther and farther back.

"So both sides finally agreed to the terms of the intermediary and I was free to finally get on with my life. I was beginning to think I was going to age into an old lady by the time the issues were resolved."

"As you should," Riko said, absentmindedly. Where exactly was Elle now? He didn't dare risk checking his phone to see if she'd replied to any of his texts or voice mails.

He had to snort a laugh. When was the last time someone had dared ignore the messages of the crown prince himself?

Gina's step faltered. "I'm sorry? I'm not sure I quite caught your meaning."

He realized he must have misspoke then made things worse by chuckling afterward.

He tried to rectify. "I mean, I'm glad all sides finally saw reason," he amended, figuring it should apply to the overall subject matter.

She seemed satisfied enough with his revision, and they continued their earlier pace. They'd fallen farther behind his parents.

"I'm sorry that I missed the first couple days of the National Spirit Festival. I do hope I get to attend many others." The innuendo in that statement wasn't lost on him.

"You can still attend this one. We've had a rain delay and will be picking up where we left off tomorrow. We still have several field races and tons of sport competitions coming up."

Gina rubbed her fingers along her throat. "I'm afraid I must come clean and admit that I'm not a terribly big fan of outdoor activities. It was the part of the trip I was least looking forward to, in fact."

She couldn't possibly mean all outdoor activities. What a dull way to go through life. "Really? You wouldn't even be enticed to participate or watch a kayak race along the river?"

"Sounds lovely," she said in a tone that was the audio equivalent of an eye roll. There was no mistaking the sarcasm in her voice.

A thought drifted into his mind. Whenever he'd encountered Gina in the past and so far into this trip, he'd always felt there was something off about the conversation. Something odd he couldn't quite put his finger on and hadn't really given much thought to. But he realized now what it was. He'd never actually seen or heard Gina laugh. The woman did have a rather pleasant smile and wore it often and well. But she never laughed. Not that he'd witnessed anyway.

He thought of Elle's lyrical laughter that first night she'd been performing the silly skit with Ramon and Tatyana. Or at Ramon's antics when she'd been dancing with him.

Just stop.

He had to stop comparing the two women. That's not what this visit was about. It wasn't what any of it was about. The simple fact was that he'd developed true feelings for Elle since meeting her.

This wasn't some sort of a competition.

Still, the realization was now clearer to him than the cloudless sky above: he was more likely to travel to the moon than spend a fulfilling lifetime with Infanta Gina Mariana De-Leon. The woman he saw by his side at next year's spirit festival was Elle. Not Gina. Not anyone else.

He'd let Gina settle for the night, but first thing tomorrow morning he would have to find his father and let him know once and for all that there would be no marriage proposal or offers of engagement being made as his parents planned for and desired.

He knew without hesitation it was the only decision that made sense. Royalty or not, mutually advantageous trade agreements or not. He was in love with someone else.

He was in love with Elle.

His mind made up, he began moving quicker than their earlier leisurely stroll. Gina didn't comment on the faster pace but kept up, and soon they were rounding the corner near the line of red leaf bushes.

His parents were several feet ahead, but they were no longer walking. His father sat perched on a nearby stone while his mother stood fanning him and mopping his brow. Concern and alarm pulsed through Riko at the sight.

"Excuse me."

He rushed to his parents.

"What's happened? Father? Are you all right?"

The king waved his hand in dismissal. "I'm fine, son. Don't go getting panicky. I just get winded sometimes these days."

These days? Did that mean this had happened before? Why was this the first Riko was hearing of it?

"Let's get the doctor down here." He reached

into his pocket for his cell phone but his mother placed a hand on his arm to stop him.

"He's already seen the doctor this morning. He just needs a minute." At Riko's hesitation, she nodded once to drive the point home.

Gina had reached them by this point.

"Is everything all right?" she asked the queen.

His mother took Gina by the arm. "Everything is fine dear. Here, why don't we continue our walk and give the king a minute to catch his breath with Riko."

Riko waited for the two women to leave before addressing his father. "What just happened?"

His dad shrugged. "Nothing in particular. Your mother was telling the truth. I'm not young anymore, son. My heart isn't what it used to be and neither are my lungs. And as privileged as we are, the life of a leader comes with many responsibilities. It takes a toll."

Riko remained silent, letting his father speak when he was ready. The king took several more deep breaths before continuing.

"I'm a tired old man, son. I just want to be able to rest and spend time with your mother before... Well, while I can."

There was a look in his father's eyes that Riko had never seen before. Fear.

The truth hit him like a ton of bricks then.

His father wasn't being obstinate about marrying Riko off. He was scared. He was trying to prepare for when he was no longer able to perform his duties. He needed Riko to be ready.

To his traditional Versuvian parents, that meant he also needed to have a queen by his side when the time came. One with experience as a leader who was known and familiar to the kingdom.

Looking at his father now, noting the utter exhaustion on the king's face, Riko realized he'd been fancifully delusional about having any real choice in the matter of his own future.

His earlier resolve about the infanta began to deflate like a pricked balloon.

She needed some air. Elle descended the circular marble staircase and walked past the kitchens to the doors that led to the back veranda.

The infanta's visit so far was going swimmingly. That's what Elle kept hearing throughout the day. She'd been witness to it herself on more than one occasion. Whenever she caught sight of Riko over the past twenty-four hours, Infanta Gina was always on his arm.

The entire palace was abuzz with speculation about how well the two of them were getting along. Elle couldn't turn down a hallway or step into a room without overhearing the gossip.

To make matters worse, Isabel had an aunt visiting today from Madrid who insisted on spending quality time alone with the children, so Elle didn't even have the benefit of the distractions they usually provided.

And every time she saw Riko and the infanta together, she died a little inside. She'd always thought that saying was so cliché. But now she knew exactly why it was worded so. Each encounter was a small stab to her heart.

She'd been wandering aimlessly but realized that she'd ended up near the maze.

Elle found the entrance and walked in. Her subconscious must have led her here. It was perfect, really. Quiet, private, away from all the talk about the prince and his potential new princess.

Still, probably better not to walk too far in. It would be all too easy to get lost. She hadn't even thought to bring her cell phone in her haste to get away from everything and everyone.

"Elle?"

She froze in her tracks, the all too familiar voice washing over her like a cold waterfall. Had Riko been behind her all this time?

Instead of answering, she rushed farther

down the pathway then took a left down another. There was nothing to say to each other. And she really didn't have it in her to discuss anything with Riko right now.

Right. As if she could fool herself into thinking that was the only reason she was avoiding him. The truth was she didn't want to look foolish by launching herself into his arms first and asking questions later.

He called out her name again, his voice coming from a parallel path. She turned the opposite direction down another opening.

"Are you still in here?" he asked softly over the wall of greenery between them. "I happened to be on the balcony and watched you enter."

It was no use. She couldn't avoid him forever. Plus there was no denying now that she was good and lost in here. She had no idea where the center or the opening was. "What do you want, Riko?"

"You've been avoiding me."

"That should have been your first clue that I wanted to be alone in here."

His soft chuckle sounded over the shrub. "Are you sure that's still what you want? I'm pretty certain you've lost your way."

He was right, damn it. There was no use

denying it. But it wasn't her fault. The blame lay with him.

"Stay where you are. I'll come find you," he said, and she heard the rustling of feet moving. Within seconds he'd rounded a corner and paused when he saw her.

She hated herself for the way her heart tugged inside her chest at the sight of him. The moon provided enough light to see him clearly. He wore dark pants and a collared shirt with the top buttons undone and sleeves rolled up to his elbows. His hair was tousled, as if he'd been ramming his fingers through it. A five o'clock shadow darkened his chin. Her fingers itched to go fix his hair then run her hand lower along his strong jawline over the stubble there. She planted her feet firmly into the ground to keep from flinging herself at him like a lovestruck fool.

"Why did you follow me, Riko? Shouldn't you be tending to your duties as a prospective groom?"

He took a hesitant step closer, like she might be a skittish doe ready to take off at the slightest fright.

She crossed her arms in front of her chest. "They're saying tonight will be the night. Actual bets are being placed."

"About?"

"When you'll propose."

He flinched, and she felt the slightest amount of satisfaction in his discomfort but it was short-lived. Nothing about this was satisfying in any way.

"Anyone who takes that bet is about to lose."

His words gave her no comfort. "Maybe. But it's just a matter of time. You can't deny it."

He tilted his head to the side. "I can't. And I won't. All I can do is ask you to understand."

He was asking too much.

"Do you remember what you were doing on your ninth birthday?" he asked suddenly, a question so random she wasn't sure if she'd heard him correctly.

"Vaguely," she answered. "Why?"

"I remember mine clearly."

"What happened?"

"Versuvia takes great pride in our national football team. That was the year we qualified for the European cup."

Soccer? How in the world were they suddenly talking about soccer?

Riko continued. "It was completely unexpected. Our team defied all odds, it was downright historical. We'd never gotten that far before. Of course, the royal family was invited to attend the tournament. It was held outside of Glasgow that year."

"I'm afraid I've never followed soccer. Or football, as you call it. And especially not when I was a child."

"Oh, I did. Manny and I were big fans. Have been our entire lives. Kicked a ball around the courtyard every chance we got."

"So you went to the tournament."

Riko shook his head. "Well, only one of us did. I was scheduled to tour a hospital with my father. My schedule was determined months in advance. Even as a child. With very little leeway to change."

Elle's heart sank for the little boy who'd had so much responsibility thrust on his shoulders at such a young age, but she wasn't grasping the reason Riko was sharing this story now. "I'm sorry, did you just compare what's happening here to a missed soccer tournament?"

He shook his head, a sad smile forming over his lips.

"No, *cariña*."

There was that word again.

"The point is, Manny got to go and I didn't. Manny got to marry the woman he loves, whereas I…" He let the sentence trail off.

Love? Had he really just uttered that loaded word in a context that included her?

It took her a moment before she could speak. "Whereas you what?"

He rammed his fingers through the hair at his crown. "Damn it, Elle. I have certain responsibilities, expectations that come with the title I was born into. About my very identity. I can't just turn my back on those responsibilities. Nor can I turn my back on the family I was born into on some kind of whim such as traveling Europe in pursuit of some dream."

His arrow hit exactly where it was supposed to. "Is that how you see me? As someone who turned her back on their family in a selfish pursuit?"

He bit out a sharp curse. "No. Of course not. That wasn't what I intended to imply."

She drew in a steadying breath. "It certainly sounded that way."

"I simply meant that duty to family has to come first to someone like me. I don't expect you to understand."

Yet another arrow. How many did he expect her to be able to deflect? How strong or uncaring did he think she was? His next words only served to amplify the question.

"It hardly matters the words I use to explain, does it? It is my truth and I must live it."

Elle sucked in a gasp at the insensitivity of the comment. Of course it mattered. It mattered deeply. To her at least. "What exactly is it that you're trying to say, Riko? Maybe you should just come out and say it."

He nodded. "Fair enough. I should have known my place, but I let my attraction for you take over. I should have never allowed myself to be alone with you. I should have never followed you up to your balcony. And I certainly should not have ever kissed you. It was all so reckless of me and I apologize."

He left unspoken the part that was shattering her soul. That he would make sure it never happened again.

Princess Isabel was looking exceptionally well when Elle checked in for their regular morning meeting five days later. Better than yesterday even and yesterday she'd looked better than the day before. Despite her inner turmoil, Elle's spirits rose ever so slightly when she entered to see her employer, who she now considered a friend, was slowly but surely on her way to a full recovery.

Elle settled into her usual chair next to the princess's bed and clicked open the app on her phone she'd been using during their daily morning meetings to take notes.

The doctor was scheduled to see her later this afternoon to give an official opinion. The family and Isabel were cautiously optimistic that she'd be given the go-ahead to resume some light activities.

There was no denying that a pressing question presented itself given Isabel's improvement. How much longer would the Suarez family even need Elle?

"I think that's it for now," Isabel said, sitting up and propping another pillow behind her back. Her next words had Elle wondering if the woman had somehow read her earlier thoughts. "Elle, I've been thinking about what a godsend you've been these past few weeks."

Elle felt a slight flutter in her chest at the compliment. With the way she was brought up, she wasn't used to people commending her performance, the only exception being her singing ability. "I'm glad I was able to help when you needed it, Isabel. And the children have become quite dear to me."

Isabel's lips spread into a wide smile. "They adore you, you know. Like a dear auntie."

The feeling was quite mutual. A lump formed at the base of Elle's throat. When her time at Palacio Suarez came to an end, she was going to miss the children the most.

Except for Riko himself, but that was a thought best left averted.

"Which is why I wanted to make sure you

knew that we're all unanimous in what I'm about to tell you."

Where was she going with this? "We've all grown quite fond of you, Elle. The Suarezes all sing your praises whenever your name comes up. Including the king and queen."

That was surprising. Riko's parents thought her praiseworthy? Right. As their nanny only. Certainly not as a potential daughter-in-law.

Whoa. She couldn't even let herself go there.

"I've become very fond of all of you as well," Elle said, recovering enough from her surprise to finally answer.

"I know your time here was meant to be temporary," Isabel said. "But we'd all like you to stay on in your role indefinitely. Again, that includes the king and queen."

Either Isabel was exaggerating the level of involvement the king and queen had in the matter or it just went to show just how little a threat the senior royal couple saw in Elle. Now that Riko's impending engagement was secure, his parents saw no reason to be concerned. If they ever were. She was probably giving herself too much credit as any kind of thorn in the royal couple's respective regal hides.

"I'm deeply honored," she replied. And she really was. But there was no way she could remain here more than a few days after Isabel was given the all-clear by her team of doctors.

It would crush her soul to imagine Riko as he proposed to the infanta, seeing his ring on her finger. Picturing the two of them say their vows. Her heart felt tight in her chest as the visions swam in her mind.

"You and your family have all been so kind. Working for you has truly been a dream job."

"I'm sensing a 'but.'"

"It's just that I've started to miss home and Chicago. And my family." That was the absolute truth. Elle was particularly missing her sisters. She'd almost called Lizzie yesterday in tears to just purge all that was happening. But her sister was in the middle of a very complicated and sensational legal case. She didn't need to worry about the baby of the family on top of all her professional responsibilities.

"That's understandable. Maybe we could arrange for a quick visit for you."

Elle's heart swelled with gratitude at the suggestion. If only things were different. If only she somehow had the ability to shut off all her emotions and simply move on. If only she hadn't fallen in love with the heir in the first place.

"Thank you, Isabel. Truly. I'll think about it."

"That's all I can ask for," Isabel answered with a gentle smile. "Thank you."

Elle left the room before the tears could begin and made her way back to her own room. The children were to read with their mother for an hour or so, leaving Elle with some time to kill.

To get some air and collect her thoughts, she stepped out onto the balcony, trying to regroup. She hadn't been out here since that night with Riko. The memory of it assaulted her and she had to wrap her arms around her middle.

For several minutes, she simply stared at the horizon, the waves in the distance, the color of the sky. Versuvia was an absolutely beautiful island. She was fortunate really to be here at all. And in due time, her heart would heal and she'd find a way to move on with just the memories of her time here. What other choice did she have?

Enough of the wallowing and self-pity. She had to shake it off.

She could at the least do something productive before it was time to go get the children. She owed several people responses to various messages so she might as well start with her texts and emails.

A note at the top of her inbox immediately caught her attention. She clicked to read the body of the email and had trouble believing what she was seeing.

...came across a video of your performance... compelling vocal range...audition at convenient time...please contact as soon as possible...

A major record label was actually seeking her out for a potential opportunity to sign with them. Completely unexpected and out of the blue.

Elle had to wonder if it was the universe giving her a sign about how to move forward.

The sign that appeared next was a lot less affable and much more jarring to her psyche. Elle stepped out of the shower and wrapped herself in the thick terry robe hanging on the back of the door, the offer from the record company still prominent in her mind.

An opportunity of a lifetime.

A knock on the door of her suite sounded just as she wrapped a thick Turkish towel around her wet hair.

Her heart pounded in her chest. Sebastian was on evening kitchen duty. The children were in bed. She wasn't expecting anyone else.

Riko.

Had he made his way back early? Had their

heated conversation in the maze been weighing on him as heavily as it had been weighing on her? Her mouth went dry as she went to answer, anticipation pounding through her veins.

But it wasn't Riko who stood on the other side when she'd flung the door open.

It was the king himself.

Elle reeled in shock. Then she cursed herself for impulsively answering the knock without so much as inquiring who it might be.

"Your Highness, my apologies," she said, absentmindedly tightening her robe belt. "I wasn't expecting anyone."

"I must be the one to apologize, young lady. I have no right to drop by so unexpectedly." True as that was, the king made no move to leave. "It was rather an impulsive decision," he added after a beat.

At a loss for anything else to do, Elle stepped aside. "Please, come in. Just give me a minute to get dressed."

The king held a hand up before she could turn to do so. "No need. This won't take long."

Something about his tone and his demeanor, added to the wholly unexpected nature of the visit, rang alarm bells through her skull. She knew without a doubt that she was wholly unprepared for anything the king might have to say to her.

"Again, I apologize for being so informal," he began, taking a step into the room and leaving the door open behind him. "But I felt it important that we spoke."

Right. Elle had no doubt that he would be doing all the speaking.

He continued. "Please understand that the extent of my family's gratitude toward you is immeasurable and eternal. I should have thanked you long before now for pulling my son out of those waters."

She could sense a colossal "but" about to follow.

"And I'd like to personally extend an invitation to you remain in our employ." As congenial as those words were, his next ones felt like a dagger to her heart. "After all, I imagine both my sons will be in need of a nanny in the following years."

Everything else that followed was completely drowned out by the roaring in her ears and the herculean effort to keep the tears stinging behind her eyes from falling. Elle could only nod, at a complete loss for any other kind of reaction.

Several minutes after he'd excused himself and left, Elle was still reeling from the king's words. So, that was to be her lot in life then if she were to remain here in Versuvia. As a nanny potentially working for the man she'd fallen in love with.

The choice before her was crystal clear.

CHAPTER TWELVE

One week later

THE SIGNS KEPT COMING.

Elle slammed the cover of her tablet shut and tossed it across the mattress. She should have known better than to go onto one of the royalty focused websites. All of Europe and many countries of the Americas couldn't get enough about the gossip regarding the Versuvian crown prince and his potential princess. Speculation was rampant on when the prince would propose to his love and how he would do it. Would it be at his castle in Versuvia, using a glass of champagne with a ring at the bottom? Or would he meet her in Barcelona, or maybe Paris, and hand her a velvet box over an elegant dinner table atop a rooftop restaurant? Maybe what the prince had in mind was much more intimate. Elle had had to stop reading the article at that point.

Where did people get all this creativity anyway?

Elle hadn't seen Riko in several days, and Isabel had hinted that he was off the island on some business or other.

Ha! That business probably involved a striking golden blonde woman of Spanish noble blood who was probably hanging on his arm at this very moment.

She desperately needed to talk to a familiar and understanding voice. With shaky fingers, she reached for her phone and dialed her sister.

Lizzie picked up immediately, alarm ringing in her voice. "Elle? What's wrong? You're never the one to call."

She sniffled. "I know. I'm so sorry about that, Lizzie. I should try and be a better sister." She should try and be a better person.

"Uh-oh. Now I'm really alarmed. Tell me."

Elle couldn't contain herself any longer. She found herself pouring out everything that had happened since the day the infanta had arrived. Starting with the heart-shattering kiss the night of the concert, the news that Isabel had gotten the medical all-clear yesterday, the things the king had said to her, to the offer of an audition from a record company and finally ending with Riko's admission of love in the maze.

At last, when Elle had finally exhausted herself and stood there panting into the phone, she heard nothing but the sound of Lizzie's breathing on the other end. Quite an accomplishment to render an attorney speechless.

"Uh, you probably should have led with that last part," her sister said at last. "You know, about how he said he's fallen in love with you." Her voice rose several octaves on the last three words.

"Oh, Lizzie. I've fallen in love with him too."

"Well, yeah," Lizzie said in a tone that had Elle envisioning exactly how she must be rolling her eyes as she spoke. "I mean, I figured that out, Elle. Let's just say one wouldn't have needed any of the private investigators the attorney's office employs to come to that conclusion."

At the mention of her sister's job, Elle immediately felt a twinge of guilt. Lizzie really had more important matters to attend to than figuratively holding her sister's hand during an emotional meltdown while over an ocean's distance away.

"Lizzie, I have to go," she said, fibbing. Her sister would never accept ending the call if she thought Elle was doing so on Lizzie's account.

What time was it even in the Midwest United States? The chances that she'd interrupted Lizzie in the middle of something important were high.

Elle wasn't in the right frame of mind to figure out time zones or do the math. It was well past midnight where she was.

"Are you sure, Elle? We can keep talking until you feel better," her sister said, further upping the homesickness she felt down to her core.

"I already do, Liz. And I love you for getting me there."

"Love you too, sis. And that prince is a fool for letting you go. You should tell him so," she added before disconnecting the call.

That wasn't going to happen. No use telling Riko any such thing at this point.

As late as it was, Elle knew the chances of her getting any sleep after such an emotional purge were slim to none. She left her room and made her way downstairs as quietly as possible so as to avoid disturbing any of the other sleeping staffers. She had to find some of the horchata Riko had offered her when he'd found out she couldn't sleep. Back when they'd been on friendly terms and were only just discovering each other.

A lifetime ago.

The kitchen was dark when she entered, covered in shadows.

One of them shifted toward the center of the room, tearing a gasp from her throat and making her jump. She wasn't alone. Her eyes finally focused enough to see Riko leaning his back against the counter with a steaming cup in his hand.

"Couldn't sleep either, huh?"

Elle had half a mind to turn around and walk back to her room. But the scent of vanilla and almond tickled her nose and ignited her taste buds.

What would be the harm in grabbing a cup and then leaving?

"I thought you were away," she said, stepping farther into the room. Even now, having him just a few feet away was wreaking havoc on her equilibrium.

She'd missed him. Achingly so.

"Returned earlier this afternoon."

She resisted the urge to ask where he'd been and with who. Or if he'd returned alone.

He reached his cup out to her. "Here, have mine. I'm not as thirsty as I thought."

If he was trying to soften her up by giving up his drink, she had to begrudgingly admit it was working. "I can't take all of it. Let's share."

"Fine. You go first."

The thought of sharing the same cup sent a jolt of desire through her center. She ignored the taunting suggestion and retrieved her own mug from the wall cabinet behind him.

He took it from her and poured in half the contents of his.

Elle took a small sip, her hands shaking at his unexpected nearness. She could only hope he didn't notice or guess the cause.

"I hear Isabel's been given the all-clear by her doctors."

She nodded. "Just this afternoon. They said she's out of the woods and can resume her old activities once more. Within reason for a pregnant woman," she added.

Riko put his cup down, turned to face her. "I also hear she would like you to stay on."

What about you? Do you want me to stay too?

Questions she desperately wanted answers to but didn't dare ask. "Yes, well, I haven't made my mind up yet. I'm still considering what I'd like to do."

"I know at least two small people who'll be sad to see you go."

He was referring to the children. A surge of anger shot through her and she slammed the cup hard enough on the counter that several drops spilled onto her hand and the surface.

"Don't, Riko. Don't try to use those kids as leverage. I've come to love and care for them deeply. My heart is going to break when I do say goodbye to them."

And it would completely shatter when she bid her final goodbye to him.

"You have to know that," she added. "And it's grossly unfair of you to try and use that knowledge in such a way."

He held both hands up as if in surrender. "That wasn't my intention. I apologize if that's how I sounded."

She didn't speak, afraid of what might leave her mouth. Equally afraid that she might just fling herself into his arms and beg him to hold her just for a few moments so that she could pretend he was hers, the way she did the night of the concert.

He rubbed a hand down his face. "I can't seem to say the right thing around you. Just like that night in the maze. Every word that comes out of my mouth seems wrong."

This had been a mistake. She should have turned right back around when she'd found him in the kitchen. At the least she should have thanked him for sharing his drink then taken it back to her room.

A mistake she could easily rectify by simply walking away.

"Good night, Riko. I hope you get some sleep."

She herself certainly wouldn't be able to.

Riko was halfway across the kitchen to chase Elle down before he stopped himself. She'd made clear twice already that she didn't want his company. Once in the maze and again when she'd come in here tonight.

It didn't help that he kept saying the wrong thing. Because he didn't know exactly what to say at all.

From what Elle knew, he'd made his choice. And he hadn't chosen her. She had no idea how much the choice had cost him. He had no way of finding the words that might help to explain. Maybe in due time, perhaps years from now, she would deign to forgive him. Until then, he should probably just leave her alone.

The door swung open again and his heart leapt with hope that she might be returning. Even if it was just to rant at him and curse him out in anger.

But it was Manny who walked into the kitchen.

"Oh, it's just you."

"Nice to see you too, big bro. How was your trip to Madrid? Did you secure the gambling licenses?"

"Fine. It went fine. What are you doing here so late?"

"Getting Isabel something to eat. That woman's appetite for food is fast approaching mine. Didn't want to bother the staff."

Riko realized he hadn't known that Manny

was so familiar with their kitchens. Whereas Elle had been the one to show Riko where the damn refrigerator was.

"Well, she is eating for two," Riko said, refocusing on the conversation.

Manny executed a dramatic flinch. "Ouch. Must have been one grueling trip. You've resorted to unoriginal cliché responses. Isabel is fine, by the way. The doctors were very pleased with her recovery. Thank you for asking."

Riko pinched the bridge of his nose. "Sorry. I'm just rather distracted at the moment."

"Does it have anything to do with the way Elle nearly barreled into me on the way out of here just now?"

"You know it does."

"Wanna talk about it?"

"No. I do not." What he wanted was to find Elle and pull her into his arms.

Manny stepped to the counter and crossed his arms in front of his chest. "Well, I think we need to."

The sudden intensity in Manny's voice caught Riko off guard. Any hint of teasing or lightheartedness was completely gone. A rarity for his brother. He walked over to the wall and switched the lights on before returning to where Riko stood.

Okay.

"I just want to ask you a couple of questions. First, are you in love with Elle?"

"I think you know the answer to that," Riko said without any preamble. "I fell in love with her sometime between overturning my boat and watching her perform a silly skit in the nursery for a king and queen she'd barely been introduced to."

Manny nodded once. "Of course I know. I just needed you to hear yourself say it out loud."

"Why is that exactly?"

Manny held up a finger. "I have one more question before you can ask any of yours."

"All right," Riko said, resigned though admittedly curious about where his brother was leading them with all this. "What's the question?"

"Are you in love with the woman you're about to propose to?"

"No." Such a simple and direct word, it had left his mouth without any thought or hesitation.

Manny spread his arms out wide. "Then what are we doing here, man? What are *you* doing?"

Was he really serious? "You know it's not that simple. Mother and Father have expectations. I can't just marry anyone I please. Unless…"

Manny dropped his arms. "Unless what?"

Riko found himself verbalizing out loud the silent thoughts that had been rumbling through his mind for a while now. Maybe even years. Thoughts that had grown louder and louder over the past few weeks since he'd met Elle. "Well, maybe we can convince the king and queen to think differently about the accession to the throne. Offer them a novel way to approach the rule of the kingdom."

Manny quirked an eyebrow. "Come again?"

"I'm to inherit the throne and I need someone by my side. Someone who can step into the role and take over Mother's duties with the experience borne of years of living a royal life."

"That's well established, big brother. So what are you getting at?"

"What if someone who isn't queen takes over Mother's duties? Someone who's had years of experience living the life of a royal. Another prince to be exact."

It took Manny a minute to process his words. Riko knew what his brother had to be thinking—that this was either the most preposterous idea in the history of the Versuvian monarchy. Or it actually had a great deal of merit.

"Are you trying to suggest that I rule by your side?"

Riko nodded. "I'm not suggesting. I'm actually saying so. I mean, come on, man. I only beat you out of the womb by a couple minutes."

"Well, when you put it that way…"

"And don't even think about attempting some sort of power grab."

Manny rolled his eyes. "Hardly. You think I want to give up this life of leisure and actually do real work on the daily?"

He was being facetious. Manny did plenty for the kingdom. He monitored the casinos and made sure the buildings were up to code, among many other tasks that involved the main national industry. But under the surface, it was a valid question.

His brother's expression suddenly grew serious. "But I'd do it for your happiness, big brother. And I know you'd do the same for me."

That was the truth. Nevertheless, Riko had to be certain. "Are you sure, Manny? This isn't something you can change your mind about later."

Manny tilted his head. "Perhaps the better question is are *you* sure? You'd be giving up the status as sole heir, if I'm hearing you correctly."

"You are," Riko said with zero hesitation.

"Have you thought this through fully?"

Riko was surprised at just how much clarity

he had about the proposal now that he'd actually spoken it out loud. "I've given it a lot of thought, in fact. We'd make sure to balance your duties as a father, of course. Especially with the arrival of the new baby."

Manny rubbed his jaw then shrugged. "Then, yes. I'm sure too. Besides, prince or not, you deserve to be with the woman you're in love with."

CHAPTER THIRTEEN

ELLE WATCHED THE blinking cursor on her screen and let her finger hover over the "enter" tab before pulling her hand back and curling it on the desk. If she clicked, she would be accepting the invitation. Once she did, there'd be no turning back.

Clicking *yes* would mean that by this time next week she'd be in New York in a recording studio in front of a group of music executives to sing an original song she'd had to compose herself. All in the hopes that it might lead to a second audition. Which in turn could mean the opportunity of a lifetime. An opportunity she'd been dreaming of since she was a little girl.

How ironic it was that she was even hesitating. If someone had told her a month or so ago that she would agonize over the decision for even a second, she would have offered to sell them the title to the Skyway Bridge.

Riko thought she had no sense of family responsibility. Well, maybe he was partially right. Maybe her father had been right all along. If she signed up for this audition, at least she'd be back in the States with her parents and sisters. But she'd be doing it on her own terms.

Without giving herself a chance to agonize any longer, she put her finger onto the key and pressed it. A confirmation box appeared on her screen almost immediately.

An odd sense of calm came over her now that she'd taken the plunge and accepted the offer. It was settled. She'd made her decision.

Riko was moving on and so would she. It had been silly and impulsive of her to be cross with him about Gina's visit. She realized that now. He was a man who'd been born into a life that came with responsibilities and expectations.

A life that couldn't and wouldn't include her.

It was time. Riko was done procrastinating. No more putting off the conversation he needed to have with his parents. He'd made his decision, and he wouldn't be turning back regardless of their displeasure.

And their displeasure would be considerable once they heard that he wouldn't be proposing to Infanta Gina, after all. Well, at least he'd be prepared to present them with something of a counteroffer, thanks to his and Manny's agreement.

Funny how a concept could linger in one's mind for decades before solidifying into a concrete idea. Incentive was all that it took apparently. Riko could think of no better incentive than the way he felt about Elle.

The idea that he and Manny could be equal partners in the ruling of the kingdom had lingered in the back of his mind for years. His feelings for Elle had finally pushed those thoughts to the surface. He had the utmost confidence that his brother would perform the royal duties equally as well as he could. No doubt there were some tasks Manny might even be better suited for. The more he thought about it, the more sense it all made.

Now, he just had to convince their parents to see reason.

He found them in their beachside cabana enjoying afternoon tea.

"What a pleasant surprise," his mother said when she saw him approach. "How lovely that you'll be joining us, son."

"To what do we owe this pleasure?" his father asked, his tone weary and suspicious. He'd obviously read Riko's expression better than the queen had.

"There's a matter I'd like to discuss with both of you," Riko began, taking an empty seat at the the teal wicker table.

The smile faded from his mother's face as she studied him. "What would that be?"

"I'd like to make an official announcement to the people of the kingdom within the coming days."

"An announcement to say what exactly?" his father demanded to know. "It had better be to declare that they may expect to hear of your engagement to the infanta."

Riko shook his head, his resolve not faltering even a little despite his father's ominous tone. "No, Father. That is not what I intend to say because it is not what I intend to do."

Their reactions were immediate. The king swore and rubbed a hand down his face. His mother's gasp was loud enough to warrant a glance from the butler several feet away.

"Riko, what is this about?" his mother asked.

Something in his chest snapped. Riko slammed both fists on the table hard enough to rattle the china and glasses. "It's about choosing how I spend the rest of my life and with whom. It's about not committing myself to a woman for eternity and hoping that I might grow fond of her."

His mother leaned back against her chair, her hand at the base of her throat. He'd shocked her. No surprise. Riko had never so much as raised his voice to either of them let alone physically acted out in their presence. Not even as a child.

The king made a noise akin to a growl and began to stand before his mother stopped him with a hand to his forearm. "Let's hear him out, dear."

Riko inhaled deeply and counted to three before attempting to begin. "As lovely as she is, I have no desire to marry Gina. And her reasons for wanting to marry me have nothing to do with affection or attraction. And certainly nothing to do with love."

His father bit out another, harsher curse before the queen patted his arm once more. "I take it you believe yourself in love with someone else," she said.

Riko could only nod. The answer had to be obvious.

The king grunted. "Love? Is that what you're after? When you have the responsibility of an entire kingdom waiting for you. Or have you forgotten?"

Riko shook his head. "No, sir. I haven't forgotten. And as far as the responsibility that awaits me, Manny and I would like to present the two of you with an idea."

Riko strode down the dock and jumped onto the hull of the new boat that had recently been delivered to replace the one the storm had wrecked all those weeks ago.

The conversation with his parents was finally behind him. And it could have gone much worse. Now he just had to find Elle and finally confess how he really felt about her.

It shocked him to learn that he was more nervous about her potential reaction than he'd been about speaking to the king and queen.

He could hardly be faulted for wanting a quick sail around the bay to clear his mind and pull his thoughts together before he searched for Elle and poured his heart to her.

An odd sense of déjà vu struck Riko as he admired the new boat. It was a beautiful, sunny and clear day. Not a cloud in the sky. Should be smooth sailing. But that's what he'd thought last time—when a singing mermaid had to come to pull him out of the stormy waves.

"Isabel told me I could find you here," a soft feminine voice sounded from behind. He turned to find Elle standing on the dock, her hand shading her eyes from the bright sun.

A sliver of alarm ran up his spine. He couldn't imagine why Elle might have sought him out after avoiding him for so long. "Is everything all right? The children—"

She cut him off with a wave of her hand. "Everything's fine."

If everything was fine, why were her eyes clouded with sadness, her shoulders rigidly tense, her breathing so shallow? He had his answer a moment later when she spoke. An answer he was loath to hear.

"I've just come to say goodbye. I've asked Seb to take me to the ferry to Majorca later this afternoon."

Riko had to take a moment to let the words sink in.

She was leaving. After everything, he was too late. And he wasn't prepared to do anything about it. He shouldn't have waited to tell Elle his plan. Now it might be too late.

Riko walked portside to where she stood, then he leaned over the railing. "What's this about, Elle? I thought you were still deciding your future plans."

She bit her lip and inhaled deeply. "I have decided due to an unexpected incentive."

"What kind of incentive?"

She wasn't making eye contact, her gaze trained off to the side toward the horizon. "I have an audition in the States. I'd like to head back and begin rehearsing. Isabel is fine now and her aunt is visiting more often. I think it's time I moved on."

Riko was stunned speechless. A barrage of

questions assaulted his mind. He couldn't even choose where to start.

"An audition?"

"With a record label. An executive came across some videos of me performing and wants me to try out for them. It sort of landed in my lap, and I don't want to pass it up."

Elle's words rushed out like water through a fire hose. They sounded rehearsed, as if she was doing her best to just get them out and get this over with. "It really is an opportunity of a lifetime," she added. "One I have to take."

"I see," was all Riko could come up with to say.

"I've already said my goodbyes to Isabel, Manny and the children. I think drawing out such partings only makes them more painful. So I'll be leaving on the next ferry to Majorca and then flying home."

Nothing about what he was feeling right now was at all painless. "An audition. That sounds like quite an opportunity. Break an arm."

She blinked up at him in confusion, then seemed to put together what he'd been trying to say. "You mean break a leg."

He didn't know what he meant. He was having trouble getting his mind to work well enough to communicate with his mouth. Elle was leaving. For good.

He'd been a fool, and he was losing the only woman he'd ever loved because he'd been too afraid to defy tradition in order to fight for that love.

"But I can take you to Majorca—" he gestured around him to indicate the boat "—whenever you'd like, *cariña.*"

She seemed to flinch at the last word. "I've already purchased the ferry ticket. And I've asked Seb to take me to the harbor. But thank you anyway."

What happened next shocked Riko into near paralysis. She boarded the boat then leaned toward him and planted the slightest peck of a kiss on his cheek, before turning on her heel and walking back toward the beach.

Riko yearned to call out to her and ask her to stay, to tell her that he'd been a fool to even entertain engaging himself to another woman when he'd fallen so completely for her.

But he stopped himself. He had no right to be that selfish. Elle said this was the opportunity of a lifetime for her.

Who was he to ask her to give it up? Especially given the way he'd messed things up so badly.

The sun had long set and the night had grown cool by the time Riko pulled back onto the dock and anchored. He'd lost track of time out on the water.

The castle was dark and quiet as he approached the front doors, the sky above it dark and moonless. Even from the outside, it appeared as if something was missing inside.

Elle was gone. When he woke up tomorrow, she wouldn't be there. She'd be well on her way to the States.

Unless she'd changed her mind. Highly unlikely. He was grasping at hope when he knew it was pointless. Still, he had to make sure.

So he bypassed his own wing and strode toward the staff quarters instead. Sure enough, her door was wide open, the room unoccupied. The bed was stripped and the closet emptied.

Riko strode inside, trailing a finger around the bureau that had once held her clothes. All the drawers were laid bare.

He could still smell her scent. Like a pathetic lovestruck character in some kind of rom-com, he inhaled deeply to savor it before it was gone for good.

A musical composition book sat in the wastebasket, otherwise empty. Riko reached in and pulled it out, flipping open to a random page in the middle. The top line said *Audition Piece*.

In between her duties with Ramon and Tatyana, Elle must have been composing an original song to use for her audition. The lyrics she'd penned immediately caught his attention.

About a woman who had fallen in love with a man she couldn't have, a man who she would never get over.

She'd entitled it "My Dear Prince."

Elle would have thought she'd be more nervous the day before an audition. But the butterflies fluttering in her stomach had nothing to do with her make-or-break performance scheduled in the city in under twenty-four hours.

No, they had everything to do with the way her mind insisted on replaying the moments that day on the dock when she'd said goodbye to Riko.

Now, sitting cross-legged on the bed in the guest room of her oldest sister's Long Island home, she tried to run through her vocal exercises one last time. But her throat felt raw and inflamed from all the effort of resisting the urge to cry.

He hadn't even tried to dissuade her from leaving. On the contrary, he'd even offered her a ride on his boat to the mainland. The memory felt like a lance through her chest.

The sobs threatened once more, and Elle knew it was no use trying to rehearse or practice. She was probably going to blow this audition, and all because she couldn't stop thinking about a man who was perhaps engaged to another woman by now.

She flopped backward onto the bed and draped an arm over her eyes. She couldn't be sure how much time had passed before her sister's voice drifted up from the first floor.

"Elle, you might want to come down here. Like now."

Elle bolted upright. That sounded rather urgent.

Shuffling down the stairs, she found her sister at the open front door, her arms crossed and her shoulders stiff.

"There. I've called her down, but I'm definitely not letting you in," Maysie was saying. "Your Highness," she added in an emphasized and accusatory tone.

The last two words had Elle's heart leaping to her throat.

"Fair enough," an all-too-familiar masculine voice answered from outside.

She rushed to the door and did a double take at the scene that greeted her.

Riko's gaze shifted from her sister to where she stood, his eyes softening when he saw her. "Elle," he said simply, the smile he gave her melting her insides.

She had no idea how, but somehow she got

her mind and mouth to work enough to speak. "It's okay, Maysie."

Her sister never tore her eyes away from Riko when she answered. "You sure?"

"Yes. It will be fine."

Her sister blew out a deep breath. "Fine. But you should remind your prince here that I happen to be very adept with sharp instruments. You know, like scalpels and such."

Elle gave her sister a one-armed hug then stepped around her to the front stoop. "I'll be okay," she assured her, though not quite certain about the truth of that statement. Her limbs had gone numb and her pulse beat like a jackhammer through her veins.

"Riko, why are you here?"

He stepped forward just enough to reach the bottom of the stone steps. Their height difference brought them eye to eye.

He was so close, the scent of him threatened to overwhelm her senses.

"I had to find you. I realized that I'd forgotten to give you something before you left. A charm you're meant to have."

What in heaven's name was he talking about? "What kind of charm?"

"For good luck. During your audition."

Elle closed her eyes and released a long sigh. Why was he really here? To toy with her by giving her some kind of trinket? He couldn't be that cruel. Could he?

"Here, I'll show you," he said, climbing the steps as he reached into the inside breast pocket of his tailored suit jacket and pulling out a delicate gold chain. She took it from him, her fingers shaking, hating that he had to have noticed. On the chain was a small gold charm. A mermaid.

Despite herself, she couldn't help but feel touched. But she knew he couldn't have traveled all this way simply to hand her jewelry, as lovely a piece as it was. Riko had to be in New York on business or something, making a detour to ensure they ultimately left each other on friendly terms.

"It's beautiful, Riko. Thank you."

"You're welcome."

She thought about inviting him in. But she just couldn't do it. It had been soul wrenching enough to say goodbye to him once. Her heart wouldn't be able to survive going through it again.

"I'll be sure to wear it when I sing tomorrow."

He simply nodded, that charming smile of his tempting every cell in her body to fling herself into his arms and ask him to hold her and never let go.

"Oh, I almost forgot," he said, and reached into his pocket once more. "I have one more good luck token that I'd like you to have."

Elle would have laughed if the situation weren't so surreal. She'd had no indication the man was so superstitious all this time. But then she saw the object in his hand and felt her jaw drop.

A black velvet box with gold trim. It couldn't...

"Arielle Stanton, I know I already owe you a world of debt considering I might not even be here if you hadn't swum into my life one fateful day. But I'd like to ask you for yet one more favor." He held the box toward her and flipped it open to reveal a glittering diamond ring. "Will you marry me?"

Elle clasped her hands to her face, doing her best to pull air into her lungs and remain upright. She just barely managed both. His name was the only word she had the ability to utter.

"I've missed you every moment since you left," he said, his voice tight and strained.

"I missed you too. So much I ached."

"I should have stopped you. I should have told you sooner, my love." The words landed like poetry to her ears. They'd wasted all this time, but he was here now.

"And I remember, Elle. I remember you

reaching for me in the water, pulling me to shore. I remember every second of it."

"You do?"

"Yes. I remember every moment we've ever been together. And I know I'll never forget."

A sliver of worry crept into her mind, threatening to mar the spirit-soaring moment. But she had to ask, had to know. "What about the infanta? What about your parents?"

"She took it well, and they've both seen reason so have given their blessing. Respectively, and in that order. Not that any of that would have made one bit of difference. I love you, Elle. And I'd be honored to call you my wife."

She believed every word. Because she felt the same. Nothing and no one would ever change how she felt about this man. How much she loved him. "I love you too. With all I have and every fiber of my being."

He reached for her then, taking her in his arms and swinging her around in a circle. "Please tell me that's a 'yes,'" he whispered in her ear, his breath hot against her cheek.

She told him without the use of any words.

EPILOGUE

The reclusive recording artist known only as Mermaid remains at the top of our charts with her debut breakout hit. "My Dear Prince" has been shattering record sales, is dominating social media, and is on track to become one of the top downloaded songs of the summer.

Reports are that all proceeds from the song are donated to various charities throughout Europe and the rest of the world. Many rumors are circulating about the identity of the artist, though none have been confirmed. For now, Mermaid remains anonymous, and there is no clue as to who she might be. Maybe one day, she'll reveal herself.

ELLE HAD NO intention of doing any such thing. She scanned the article on her tablet screen with a smile, hardly able to believe those words were actually about her. It was a true marvel just how much her life had changed since she'd first arrived on the Spanish coast two years ago.

There was no reason to divulge to the world that she was the voice behind this summer's top hit. Her life as it was happened to be more than she could have ever hoped for.

The man mostly responsible for that idyllic perfection strode onto the veranda just then and dropped a kiss on her cheek before pulling out a chair to sit down next to her.

"We might have a problem," he announced, handing her a fresh cup of *horchata*. His teasing tone indicated the "problem" wasn't all that serious.

"We do?"

He nodded. "Yes. Ramon and Tatyana are begging me to use all my royal connections and clout to find out who Mermaid is and invite her to perform at this year's National Spirit Festival."

"Hmm, that is a problem."

The children were simply too young to be trusted with the truth. In due time, she would tell them that their former nanny and current aunt had written the song they both sang along to and hummed incessantly during the day.

But right now, she couldn't risk her secret getting out.

"Speaking of the festival, we've received a few more RSVPs," Elle informed him. "Infanta Gina will be attending."

Not only had the infanta graciously accepted the fact that she would not become the next Princess Suarez, the infanta had actually admitted to feeling relief that the nuptials had fallen through so that she may focus on pursuing a career in politics.

Riko didn't get a chance to respond to Elle. Suddenly, without any warning, the sky above turned dark as night and spiderwebs of lightning lit the air. A roar of thunder echoed around them.

"Where'd that come from?" Riko asked, moving to help her up so that they could run inside out of the storm.

Elle shook her head, taking his hand and pulling him down for a long lingering kiss.

"I'd like to stay out here," she said, breathless after reluctantly pulling away.

Riko didn't argue, gave her a knowing smile instead. He had to have guessed where her thoughts had gone.

She didn't mind the rain, thunder and lightning in the least. In fact, it was a good omen of what was to come as far as Elle was concerned.

After all, if it hadn't been for an unexpected storm one otherwise bright and sunny day, Elle would have never found the man who'd become the most cherished part of her world.

* * * * *

*If you enjoyed this story,
check out these other great reads
from Nina Singh!*

The Prince's Safari Temptation
Two Weeks to Tempt the Tycoon
Caribbean Contract with Her Boss
Reunited Under the Tuscan Sky

All available now!